SHADOW COLLATERAL

THE SHADOW AGENCY
BOOK 4

CHRISTY BARRITT

KAI KALEO TOSSED his empty coffee cup into a trashcan on the bustling DC sidewalk and paused near the curb.

His muscles tightened, and the hair on his neck rose. He pushed his sunglasses higher, determined not to change his demeanor and show he was on guard.

But someone was watching him. He was certain of it.

Years of training and experience had finely tuned his instincts.

Remaining casual, he glanced across the street as vehicles zoomed by in the afternoon rush.

He spotted her.

A woman stood at the edge of the office building across the street. Her dark hair fell into her eyes, hiding some of her features. Her black T-shirt and sunglasses concealed the rest.

But Kai knew she was watching him.

His fists tightened.

Had one of his enemies sent her? Plenty of people had valid reasons for wanting to take him down.

But this woman didn't look threatening—at least not from this distance. She appeared too soft, too nervous. But that didn't mean she wasn't dangerous.

As Kai waited with throngs of professionals for the light to change, his gaze skimmed behind her.

Two men stood farther down the street, each looking at their cell phones as if trying to appear casual.

But their stiff motions and quick glances showed they were also watching.

Based on the bulge of the guns beneath their shirts and their fit physique, they meant trouble.

There were three of them. Three people watching Kai.

He needed to figure out what they wanted. But here on the busy sidewalk with so many bystanders wasn't the place to do so.

A plan formed in his mind.

Remaining casual, he tucked his hands into the pockets of his leather jacket as the traffic light changed, giving him permission to walk. He crossed the street and strode down the sidewalk, keeping pace with those around him.

The smell of the city surrounded him—hot dogs from a stand on the corner, exhaust from cars, and some perfume from a nearby shop. When he peered up at the right angle, he could see the Washington Monument on occasion.

He denied himself the urge to look over his shoulder and see if the woman was still following.

Kai knew she was. He just didn't know how close.

As he passed a car parked on the side of the street, he glanced into the sideview mirror.

There she was. Ten feet behind him. Still trailing.

He couldn't see the two goons with her. Right now, he'd only focus on the woman.

He walked another block before reaching a retail area. He turned into an alley between an upscale greasy spoon and a hotel often frequented by politicians. The space was narrow and dark, lined with three dumpsters and a fire escape.

If the woman followed him this way, as Kai predicted she would, it would be the perfect opportunity to have a little talk with her and find out what she wanted.

Kai needed to turn the tables on her.

He ducked behind a dumpster and waited.

A moment later, the soft thud of tennis shoes sounded.

It was her. His plan had worked.

Kai held his breath, his body locked and loaded as he prepared to act.

He listened closely to her footsteps.

The woman reached the dumpster. Probably six more strides, and she'd be in front of him. Then he'd make his move.

He counted the steps.

One.

Two.

Three.

Four.

Five.

He sprang from the shadows and grabbed the woman's wrists.

She cried out as if his sudden appearance had scared her. Before she could fight back, Kai pinned her hands behind her and shoved her against the brick wall of the restaurant.

"Who are you?" he demanded. "Why are you following me?"

"Please, don't hurt me!" Her voice shook with fear.

Good. He wanted to scare her.

Yet something about her reaction didn't fit the image he'd developed in his mind of this woman.

Operatives who worked for his enemy didn't get

scared. Unless this was all an act, an effort to get him to let down his guard.

He had to be careful.

What exactly was she up to?

Kai needed to find out the answers.

Now.

———

Tori Bristow's pulse surged as fear swept through her.

She was going to die right now, wasn't she? This man—Kai Kaleo—wanted to kill her.

Please, Lord. Help me!

The rough ridges of the brick wall dug into her face, and her cheek stung with pain. Smelly dumpsters stood on either side of her. And a man—maybe a deadly operative—held her at his mercy.

"Who are you, and what do you want?" Kai demanded, his tone hard and unyielding.

"Please." Her voice trembled. "Don't hurt me."

Tori had no idea when she began shadowing him that he'd be violent or put her in this position.

"I asked who you are," he repeated. "And why are you following me?"

"I . . . I just want to talk."

"Talk?" He nearly scoffed as he repeated the word. "Who sent you?"

"No . . . no one." What was he talking about? Were others trying to find him as well? "I don't know what you mean. I came on my own accord."

"Stop playing dumb. I'm not falling for your act."

His hot breath hit her ear as he leaned into her, and the subtle scent of his leathery aftershave broke through the putrid smell of trash.

"This isn't an act. I just want to talk." Tori had to convince him she was telling the truth. If she didn't . . . she could only imagine what this man might do.

"Then why didn't you just approach me instead of trying to be sneaky?"

The reasons slammed into her mind. Tori had clearly put herself in a dangerous position. But she'd never imagined this . . . she'd only wanted answers.

"I didn't know if I could trust you." Her voice sounded strained, even to her own ears. "I didn't know if you were a good guy or a bad guy. I . . . I still don't know. You're hurting me."

Her cheek continued to sting as he kept her pressed against the rough bricks.

Kai's grip loosened slightly. "Fine. I'm going to release you. But one wrong move and you're right back up against the wall . . . understand?"

"I understand." Her voice squeaked.

He released her.

Slowly, Tori turned around, rubbing her wrists where his hands had clamped onto her.

Her life depended on her doing as Kai asked.

She raised her hands in the air to prove she wasn't a threat.

Then she observed Kai a moment—this time up close instead of from a distance. The man appeared part Asian with broad shoulders and a strong build. Just under six feet tall. Perceptive brown eyes. Thick, dark hair. He'd taken off his sunglasses—just as she had when she entered the dark alley.

She'd placed them in her shirt pocket, but she had a feeling they were busted now.

The man's nostrils flared, and his eyes grew steely as he stared her down. "Start talking. My patience is running thin."

Tori swallowed hard before saying, "I don't mean any harm. I just didn't know who else to turn to."

His eyes narrowed. "Turn to about what?"

"My brother died two weeks ago." Her voice trembled. "I've been trying to find answers about what really happened to him. That search for answers led me to you."

Kai shook his head, and his brows lifted as if he hadn't expected her words. "Who was your brother?"

"Nathan Bristow, and my name is Tori Bristow."

Some of the confusion left his gaze, replaced with more agitation. "Never heard of him."

He was about to manhandle her again, wasn't he?

"No!" She raised her hands in front of her and braced herself. "Please!"

But Kai didn't touch her. Instead, his jaw twitched as he stared at her. "I'm going to need more of an explanation than that."

"I'd love to talk to you about it. But not like this. Not here. Please." The isolated location felt too risky. Her pulse roared in her ears as her blood pressure climbed.

His gaze remained hard. "Who are those two guys with you?"

"What two guys?" Tori glanced around, her eyes widening with fear. "I don't have anyone with me."

She didn't see anyone else in the alley. So what was he talking about?

She'd come here to DC alone. She hadn't told a soul.

She had no one to tell, especially now that her engagement had ended.

"Don't lie to me," Kai growled. "I saw those two men shadowing you. Are they your backup?"

Shakes overtook her limbs. Tori had no idea what he was talking about. But she didn't like the implications.

"I'm telling you the truth," she stammered. "It's just me. If men are following me . . . it's not because I asked them to."

Kai stiffened with realization and glanced at the end of the alley. Tori followed his gaze.

The silhouettes of two men appeared near the street.

Fear clutched Tori with such force she could hardly breathe.

She felt certain she'd never seen those men before.

But she knew one thing for sure.

She was in trouble.

Kai seemed to agree as he grabbed her arm. "We've got to get out of here."

CHAPTER
TWO

KAI BELIEVED the woman in front of him didn't know those guys.

She looked truly terrified with her wide eyes and shallow breaths.

Were they following her, knowing she was looking for Kai?

Or was this all about the woman?

As the questions ran through his mind, the men strode toward them. If he and Tori were going to get away, then they needed to move. Now.

"You're going to have to trust me." Kai grabbed her arm and pulled her in the opposite direction of the men. "Come on."

Fear flittered through her eyes, but she didn't resist. Thankfully, she was light on her feet and quick.

"Hey!" one of the men behind them called. "Stop right there!"

No way was Kai stopping.

He knew trouble when he saw it. Those men were *definitely* trouble.

Tori, on the other hand . . . he was still on the fence about her. She might be trouble, but she was also *in* trouble. He'd have to sort through the details later.

The two of them reached the end of the alley, and Kai headed left toward a more populated area. They'd have better opportunities to lose these guys in a crowd.

"You have no idea who those men are?" Kai called over his shoulder to Tori as they ran.

"I've never seen them before in my life. How long have they been following me?"

"At least for the last fifteen minutes."

"You knew I was following you for fifteen minutes?" Surprise laced her voice.

"You were pretty obvious." Kai stopped at the street and glanced to the left and the right.

He made a split-second decision to head right.

As they hurried down the sidewalk, Kai stole a glance over his shoulder.

The men emerged from the alley like soldiers on a mission.

Kai knew he and Tori only had a moment to lose

these guys. He pulled her into a nearby men's clothing store.

"Look casual," he murmured as he led her away from the door toward the back of the store.

Tori nodded. Despite her promise, her entire body appeared tense. Not to mention how her eyes were too wide and her breathing too shallow.

Anyone looking at them would clearly know something was wrong.

"Can I help you?" A sales lady turned to them with a superficial smile as she glanced them up and down.

"We're just browsing." Kai forced a smile. "But thank you."

He led Tori toward the back of the store, briefly pausing to pretend to check out a Hawaiian-style shirt. Really, he was waiting for the sales lady to stop watching them.

As soon as he saw the woman turn to address another customer, he pulled Tori to the back of the store into an Employees Only area.

A woman on lunch break looked up from a table where her sandwich and chips were spread out on a napkin. "This isn't for the public."

"Whoops." Kai shrugged as if clueless. "Sorry."

Before she could say anything else, he shoved open an exit door and ran outside. He and Tori had no time to waste.

He didn't know where those men were. Didn't know if they'd gone into the store or not.

But he couldn't take any chances.

"This way!" He pulled Tori down another alleyway toward a fence at the end.

"We're going to be trapped!" Tori uttered, her steps slowing.

"We've got this." He paused at the chain link barrier and cupped his hands, holding them low. "Put your foot in my hand. I'm going to boost you over."

She glanced at the nine-foot-high fence then at herself in her jeans, T-shirt, sneakers, and crossbody bag. "But . . ."

"You can do it. You have to do it."

She stared at him for only a split second and then nodded. The next instant, she slipped her foot into his hands, and he boosted her over.

Her ascent and descent weren't necessarily graceful, but Tori made it to the other side. Thankfully, the top of the fence was smooth and not adorned with razor-sharp barbed wire.

Kai easily climbed the fence and landed with the agility of a gymnast on his feet beside her.

If only they could take a breather here. But they couldn't.

They darted down another alley and into another building—a candy store this time.

As soon as they stepped inside, Kai drew in a deep breath and reminded himself to look casual. They strolled toward the front, Kai keeping his eyes open for any signs of danger. So far, the only danger was future diabetes.

The scent of sugar and artificial fruit made his mind slam back in time to when his father—trying to get on Kai's good side—had taken him shopping. He'd bought him a half pound of Sour Patch Kids.

Kai, for the longest time, had considered that the best day of his life.

He and Tori sauntered through displays of colorful lollipops and bins of candy by the bulk, trying to look like tourists. Finally, they reached the front door—one that was surrounded by clouds of cotton candy and rainbow candy garlands.

As they stepped outside, he scanned the street and sidewalk.

There were no signs of those guys anywhere.

But that didn't mean he and Tori were out of danger yet.

They would need to proceed with caution.

And Kai needed to figure out who this Nathan Bristow guy was.

———

Tori's lungs burned as she tried to catch her breath—all while trying not to show just how winded she was. Showing too much weakness might put her at risk even more, and she still wasn't sure if she could trust Kai.

"This way." Kai led her across the street.

As he did, Tori scanned the area for any signs of those men.

She didn't see them.

Not yet.

She halfway expected them to reappear at any moment.

Instead of running more, Kai pushed open the door to a Vietnamese restaurant. A woman at the hostess desk greeted them. Kai said something to her in another language, and the woman responded before nodding toward the back of the restaurant.

Kai led her to a seat just out of sight of the entrance. An extravagant bamboo lattice provided them a view of the front windows while also concealing them.

Perfect.

Kai sat facing the door, his eyes still alert.

Hesitantly, Tori slid into a chair beside him. She didn't want her back to the door either.

Not until she knew what was going on.

Before Kai could ask any questions, the hostess appeared again with two glasses of water. She and

Kai had another conversation, clearly familiar with each other. His fluent use of another language was impressive.

Nathan had also been fluent in Spanish, German, and Chinese—that she knew about. There could have been others.

"I hope you don't mind, but I ordered some tea and soup for you," Kai said when the woman left. "I told her we didn't want anything, but she wouldn't take no for an answer."

"What if I do mind?" Tori raised an eyebrow, though she knew this wasn't the time to be sassy.

"Then I apologize. But we have a lot to talk about."

Yes, they did. Tori couldn't deny the truth in his words.

She'd traveled a long way and gone through a lot to find him. She'd been trying to get a feel for him before this had happened. In retrospect, maybe she should have been direct. But she hadn't been sure if she could trust him or not.

"Now do you want to tell me who you are?" Kai shifted toward her, his intense gaze burning into hers.

She drew in a deep breath. Though she'd been imagining this conversation for a while, she suddenly didn't know where to start. "I believe you knew my brother."

"I didn't know any Nathans." His voice sounded clipped and all-business. "Why would you think I did?"

"If you don't mind me starting from the beginning . . . I'm a traveling nurse based out of Florida, but I've been working in Seattle for the past four months. While I was there, I got word that my brother had died of cardiac arrest."

His gaze softened. "I'm sorry to hear that."

"Me too." Tori pressed her eyes closed at the memory but tried to keep her emotions at bay. She didn't have time to let her grief emerge right now. "I went straight to Atlanta from Seattle for his funeral, and I stayed there a week to try to get his affairs settled."

Just then, the waitress delivered their tea and soup. She also brought rice, a plate of veggies, and some spring rolls.

Kai and the woman talked back and forth for several minutes, and Tori could only imagine what their conversation was about.

"You shouldn't have."

"A young strapping man such as yourself should eat."

"We can't stay long."

"You can stay long enough."

Tori had always loved the hospitality of Asian cultures, and she could read the woman's body language enough to interpret that much.

Whatever the conversation, the food smelled wonderful, like clove and coriander.

Too bad she had no appetite.

When the waitress left, Kai turned back to her. "Hanh will be personally insulted if we don't eat this, even though I told her we weren't that hungry. At least pretend to eat a spring roll."

"I can do that." She lifted a roll into her hands.

"You were saying?"

Tori swallowed hard before continuing. "After working on things at Nathan's place, I headed home to Florida instead of going back to Seattle. My job was ending there anyway, and I needed a few days by myself to process my grief. When I got home, I found a package inside my house."

"Inside?" Curiosity gleamed in Kai's gaze.

"Yes, in my oven, actually," Tori said. "My mom caught the house on fire when we were younger because she'd stored some papers in the oven. Ever since then, I always check the inside before turning it on. Paranoia? Maybe."

"But your brother knew you did that."

"Exactly. I don't have a roommate, so I was startled at first. Besides, all my mail had been forwarded to Seattle, so it didn't make sense . . . but my name was handwritten on the package—in my brother's handwriting." She paused. "Then I opened it, and things made more sense. Nathan must have delivered it and figured out a way to get inside. He was always resourceful like that."

"What was inside the package?" He picked up a spring roll and took a bite. "Must have been pretty important."

"Handwritten notes." Tori dug into her crossbody bag and pulled out a manilla envelope. "He explained his reasoning for being so secretive in a note he left in the package. Said he couldn't risk typing what he had to say, that his computer was being monitored."

Kai narrowed his eyes as he studied the package in her hand.

He didn't, however, ask to see what was inside.

Instead, he asked, "Was he paranoid?"

"I don't think so. Nathan told me how he'd been a part of a secret government project to create what was essentially a super soldier. Told me he was put through rigorous training and classes. That he went through experiments and tests. That they even gave him drugs to enhance certain abilities."

Kai's expression remained unreadable. "I'm not saying his words have any merit, but was that the first time he'd said something like that?"

"Yes, it was. I knew he was special forces, but that was the first I'd heard about these . . . experiments." She frowned as she imagined what he might have been through. "Anyway, he went on to say that he'd started questioning things. That those above him didn't appreciate it. Then he said he feared they might kill him to keep his silence." Tori's throat burned as she said the words.

Kai shifted beside her, his expression not giving any hints as to what he was thinking or if he was familiar with what she said or if any of this surprised him.

There was nothing.

"So you're telling me that you believe your brother was part of a top-secret military program and that this program ultimately got him killed?" Kai said. "And that the leaders covered up his death in order to keep their noses clean?"

She knew it sounded crazy, but Tori didn't blink as she stared at him. "Yes, that's exactly what I am saying."

KAI TRIED to keep his expression neutral. But his mind raced as he tried not to stare at the yellow envelope on the table. He didn't want to seem too anxious to see what was inside.

How did Tori know those details she'd just shared?

No one knew about the secret program he'd been a part of—only the people who were directly involved. And Kai knew each of them. They were a small, close-knit community.

Everyone who'd participated had been unattached. The military had purposefully chosen men without strong family or community ties. Men who didn't have anyone to miss them if something happened.

But this Nathan guy had clearly had Tori. He didn't fit the profile.

However, everything else she'd said did fit. They were things other people weren't supposed to know about.

Kai's stomach churned as he tried to make sense of everything she'd told him.

Tori took a sip of her soup, but her eyes remained apprehensive as she waited for his response.

His gaze went to the yellow envelope again, but he used his self-control and didn't touch it still. Besides, the documents inside could have been forged.

However, Tori had risked a lot to come here and find him.

He wanted to believe her. But what if she wasn't telling the truth? What if she was a plant? Someone who'd been sent to test his loyalty?

It was a possibility. He wouldn't put anything past Alan Larchmont, his boss.

Even though Kai and his teammates weren't officially part of Project Elevate anymore, Larchmont treated them as if they were. Each time one of his colleagues had tried to engage in any type of relationship, Larchmont protested.

Thankfully, his colleagues hadn't capitulated. But Larchmont was putting even more pressure on the rest of them. He clearly wanted to keep them under his thumb, and he didn't like the fact he was beginning to lose control.

So what about this Nathan Bristow guy?

And who exactly was this Tori woman sitting in front of him? Who were the men chasing her?

Kai needed to figure out his next play.

"You don't believe me." Something glimmered in Tori's eyes—a deep emotion, pleading, maybe even desperation. "Why would I go through all this trouble to find you just to lie?"

"I can think of many reasons, actually. But I'm telling you the truth when I say I didn't know your brother. I'm sorry you've gone through all this for nothing."

"Don't tell me this was for nothing." Her hand hit the table, and her soup leapt from its bowl.

The hostess glanced at them, and Tori murmured an apology.

"Don't make a scene," Kai warned.

"Sorry." Tori took a deep breath. But her words still sounded charged as she said, "Something happened to Nathan, and I *will* find answers—with or without you."

Kai studied her. The woman seemed so sincere, not like the type to pull the wool over his eyes, so to speak. But he'd learned to trust no one. In his world, everyone had ulterior motives. Had reasons to use him.

Especially women.

"Nathan left your name and photo in that packet," Tori continued. "And your work address. So I bought a plane ticket here. After landing at the airport, I dropped my things off at my hotel and then caught the Metro to downtown. I was about to go to your office when I saw you leaving. I decided to follow you a moment to see what you were like before I approached . . ."

More details fell into place.

He glanced at her and realized she was hardly breathing as she waited for him to say something—to possibly confirm that he believed her words were true.

He didn't know this Nathan guy. But he was intrigued.

How else would Tori know the things she did? What else was in that packet? What exactly did she want his help with?

This whole situation spelled trouble, and Kai still wasn't sure if he could trust her or not.

He swallowed hard. His best bet right now was to stick with his cover story.

"I can't help you," Kai finally said. "I'm a security contractor, but that's it."

"Then why did Nathan mention your name and address in the papers he left for me?"

Kai shrugged and kept his expression neutral. "What's your theory?"

"He said he was searching for other people like him. People that had been through this top-secret program. He thought he'd found information that led to you. He hoped that you might have answers, but he never had the chance to find you. That's why I tracked you down instead."

"I'm sorry you went through all this trouble, but—"

Tori grabbed his hand. "Please, don't dismiss me. If you don't help me, I don't know who will."

Fire raced through Kai at her touch—fire so hot he reactively pulled away.

Her cheeks flushed, and she lowered her hand into her lap as if she hadn't meant to touch him. As if she felt self-conscious of his rejection.

He kept his expression placid. "There's got to be someone else you can talk to. Are you saying my name was the only one your brother mentioned?"

"There was one other name, but this person is unreachable. There's no way I can get to him. Besides . . . Nathan mentioned him as a suspect in the death of one of his friends. If this guy could kill my brother's friend—and then my brother—then he could definitely kill me."

Kai went still. "Who was that guy?"

"A man named Alan Larchmont. He's supposedly in charge of the program that got my brother killed."

Larchmont? Kai's eyes narrowed.

Maybe this woman *was* telling the truth.

But if that was the case, his whole world was about to turn upside down.

———

As soon as Tori said Larchmont's name, she saw the flash of recognition in Kai's gaze.

He couldn't deny what she'd said anymore. Even if he did, she'd seen the truth in his eyes.

Now she waited to see if he'd help. If he said no, she didn't know what she'd do.

As the seconds ticked by, her mind drifted back to the men who'd been trailing her through the streets of DC. She had no idea who they were. She only knew her life would never go back to normal—if she lived long enough to see the future.

Kai shifted, his gaze heavy with thought—yet carefully guarding his emotions.

She waited more.

Finally, he said, "I don't know if anything your brother said was true or not. He could have been having some type of mental break or—"

"Mental break?" Her voice climbed higher. "Are you kidding me? People who have mental breaks don't give those kinds of details. He wouldn't have specifically mentioned your name. You're trying to deflect from the truth."

He opened his mouth and then shut it again. Finally, he said, "I'm sorry. I should have been more sensitive."

"Thank you."

"Either way, I'm intrigued. I'll see what I can find out for you."

Tears rushed to her eyes at his words. "You will?"

Kai's expression tightened again as if an emotional wall had gone up after her reaction. "But to be clear, I don't trust you, and I'm not saying I agree with anything you've said. However, I will try to find out more."

"That's all I want."

Maybe Tori would finally get some answers as to what had happened to her brother. She'd done all she could on her own and knew she needed help—help from someone on the inside.

Help from someone like Kai.

She forced herself to take a couple more bites of her food. Though the spring roll and soup was delicious, her appetite was gone.

Kai reached for the package. "May I?"

She nodded, though nausea squeezed her insides.

But as he reached for the envelope, he paused and stiffened as if something were wrong.

Tori followed his gaze out the window. She didn't see anything except shoppers and tourists. Busy professionals. Taxis and cars. A mailman.

Nothing of concern.

Then she sucked in a breath as someone across the street came into focus.

Two someones.

The two men who'd been chasing them.

They were outside the restaurant looking this way.

At any second, those guys might find her and Kai.

And Tori might be permanently silenced . . . just like her brother.

KAI DROPPED some cash on the table and stood.

"We've got to get out of here. Now." He took Tori's hand and started toward the back of the restaurant.

Before he pulled her too far, Tori grabbed the envelope and stuffed it back into her bag.

She didn't bother to argue. Clearly, she'd seen those men also.

As he'd done earlier, Kai pulled her out the back door and into the alley. Instead of running to the end of the narrow corridor, he opened the door to the shop next door.

A coffee shop.

"Look casual," he murmured as they stepped inside.

They passed some bathrooms. A display of

pastries. A coffee prep area. Random wooden tables and chairs filled with patrons.

No one gave them a second look.

Good.

He kept pulling Tori toward the front door. He needed to see if those men had gone into the Vietnamese restaurant or if they'd continued down the street.

He paused by the front window but didn't see them.

This was their cue to leave. Now.

He and Tori had to somehow get to his SUV before those men spotted them.

Kai pulled Tori out the door and headed away from the restaurant. He needed to put enough space between them that they wouldn't be spotted again.

Just as they turned left, someone behind them yelled, "Stop!"

Those men had found them after all.

"Run!" he told Tori.

They sprinted down the sidewalk, dodging other pedestrians, until they reached a crosswalk.

The light changed to a red hand indicating for them to stop—but they kept going.

Cars blasted their horns as the drivers threw on brakes.

Kai raised his hand and murmured, "Sorry."

But he wasn't sorry.

He was in survival mode. He'd do whatever it took to get to safety and find out some answers.

As he and Tori reached the end of the next block, he prayed he'd lost those guys.

He glanced behind them again.

No such luck, he realized, his stomach sinking.

The thugs were still there, still on their heels.

Not only that, but they seemed to be gaining on them.

Kai needed to think of an alternate plan.

He quickly scanned the street in front of them.

An idea hit him.

Holding on to Tori's hand, he darted toward a taxi waiting at the corner. He opened the back door and shoved Tori inside.

"We need to go." Kai's palm slapped the seat to get the driver's attention. "Now."

The taxi driver looked at him in the rearview mirror, eyes narrowed with annoyance. "Who do you think I am? A—"

"Take this." Kai handed him a fifty.

The money got the guy's attention. "Here we go."

As the light changed, the driver peeled away.

Kai looked behind him in time to see the two men stop and look for their own taxi.

Thankfully, Kai didn't see any other vehicles around.

But it was too soon to let down his guard.

———

Tori's heart continued to race. She glanced out the window at those men and waited to see if they would reach another taxi before she and Kai took off.

They didn't.

But that didn't mean she could relax. There was still a chance the men could jump into another car and catch up with them.

She kept watching the men.

But they didn't jump inside and commandeer any other vehicles.

She swerved her gaze forward and saw the stream of traffic continued moving. No cars stopped.

Maybe she and Kai had gotten away.

But how long would this reprieve last? Would the men find them again?

Kai rattled off directions to the driver, and they continued down the busy street.

After a few minutes, he settled back in his seat, seeming to relax a moment. "I think we're safe. For now."

Tori let out a long breath.

But she knew all it would take was one traffic jam or red light, and those guys could catch up.

Please, Lord, don't let that be the case. Please.

Just as she whispered a silent amen, Kai turned to

her. "You really have no idea who those men are, do you?"

"I have no idea."

"Today is the first time you've seen them?"

"Yes," she told him, wishing he wasn't so skeptical of everything she said. "I had no idea they were following me. I thought I was pretty observant, but . . . I guess not."

She watched Kai, saw that he was still assessing the situation. The man was clearly smart and an experienced soldier—just like her brother had been.

At the thought, her throat burned. She missed Nathan so much. She missed trying out new restaurants with him—their most recent kick had been anything Italian. She missed playing Catan together, even though he always beat her. She missed their inside jokes.

She swallowed back her tears and asked, "Where exactly are we going?"

She'd taken the Metro into the downtown area, and she didn't know DC well enough to have a good sense of where they were.

"I'm trying to figure out our final destination." Kai stared out the windshield, his face stoic. "I don't know who I can trust right now."

His words lingered in the air before finally settling with unease in her gut. What did that mean?

Did he suspect someone he knew might not be trust-worthy? And if so, why?

Tori didn't know him well enough to ask those questions. Instead, she leaned back in the seat and tried to calm her racing thoughts.

She would need every ounce of her energy later . . . especially if those men found her again.

KAI'S THOUGHTS continued to race as they headed out of the city.

What if Larchmont really had commissioned the murder of one of his operatives?

Kai had never heard of this Nathan guy. But some information was on a need-to-know basis. He was in the dark about many aspects of the program he'd endured.

But what if the facts were worse than he'd ever imagined?

He didn't want to ask those questions. But it was imperative that he did. Unless he knew the truth, he would never truly be free.

Most of his life he'd been an obedient little soldier. He'd done whatever was required. He'd been programmed to be that way.

He'd been through experiments, through medical trials, through rigorous physical and mental training to become the best of the best. Sometimes he wondered if what he'd been through was morally sound or even legal.

Those weren't the only things included in this program. He'd also been taught multiple languages and an array of miscellaneous skills like cooking and falconry and auto repair. He'd been on covert missions all over the world, missions where he needed to act as a shadow. Missions where, if he was caught, the US government would deny knowing him.

Then the program ended, and he'd been left to adjust to civilian life—in a manner of speaking, at least. He was no longer officially military, but the ties still remained strong.

He knew one thing from his experiences: He had no room in his life for love or a family. Normal wasn't a possibility—not after everything he'd learned and done.

Sure, Kai had volunteered to participate in the program. But he'd been fresh out of high school when recruited. The program had been painted in such a positive light that he'd truly had no idea what he was getting himself into.

By the time he knew, it was too late. He'd vacillated between feeling honored to have been chosen and feeling trapped. If he could go back and do it again . . . he would have said no.

He crossed his arms over his chest as tension threaded through him.

He needed help if he wanted to get through this. He thought about his teammates. Thought about who he could trust.

A few names came to mind. But one came to the forefront.

Gage Pearson. His colleague was smart, trustworthy, and working an assignment only two hours south of DC in Richmond. It was only a surveillance gig—nothing too pressing.

Maybe he would ask Gage for some help. Kai liked to think he could do this alone, but he knew that wasn't true. Plus, he remembered the Bible verse from Ecclesiastes 4:12. "Though one may be overpowered, two can defend themselves. A cord of three strands is not quickly broken."

He'd found that to be true. He'd been trained to be independent. But sometimes, it was necessary to get other opinions. To have someone watching your back. To know there were others you could depend on.

Without thinking about it anymore, Kai grabbed his phone and called Gage. He'd need help securing a hotel, especially if he wanted to do it off the books.

He didn't think his bank cards were being traced.

But he couldn't take the chance—particularly if Larchmont might be involved.

Gage would have the resources to do what was needed without being caught.

Kai would have his colleague rent a room.

Then Kai and Tori would head to the hotel. Once there, he and Tori needed to have a serious talk, and Kai would have to make some big decisions—decisions that could impact his future.

———

Tori tried to quell her anxiety, but the task felt nearly impossible. Too many things ran through her mind.

The biggest one being the immediate threat on her life.

She'd been through a lot of challenges in her twenty-eight years. But being on the run had never been one of them.

Her brother's image drifted through her mind.

She was doing this for him. For Nathan. She couldn't give up. He deserved better than that. If he'd been killed, then whoever was responsible needed to be brought to justice.

The taxi pulled up to a hotel about an hour outside DC. Tori wished she'd been paying more attention. Wished she knew if she and Kai had traveled north or south or west.

But she had no idea where they were. She only knew the population wasn't as dense here. The buildings weren't as close. They had to be somewhere in Northern Virginia. It was the only area that made sense.

Kai paid the driver. Later, Tori would need to think of a way to pay him back. She hadn't known things would escalate so quickly or she might have considered these scenarios earlier and planned for them.

Then Kai escorted her into a room on the second floor of an upscale chain hotel that appeared to have been recently renovated. It even smelled clean.

She froze when she saw a tall man with dark hair and a five o'clock shadow waiting inside for them.

"It's okay," Kai said. "He's with me. Tori, this is my friend I was speaking to on the phone. Gage. Gage, Tori."

The two of them exchanged a stiff nod.

If Kai trusted this man, then she needed to also. She was out of options.

"Why don't you have a seat?" Kai pointed toward a table in the corner with chairs tucked underneath.

She pulled out a chair and lowered herself there.

Gage pushed a bottle of water toward her. "You might need this."

She twisted the cap off and took a long sip, not realizing how thirsty she was. All the running and anxiety—and maybe even the salty soup—had dehydrated her.

When she put the bottle down, both men still stared at her.

"I need you to tell us everything." Kai crossed his arms, all business. "Even if you've already told me, I need you to tell me again. So Gage can hear."

The request seemed fair enough, all things considered.

She went through the story. Told them how Nathan had died. How she suspected that someone he worked with—or for—had secretly killed him. How she'd managed to track Kai down. How she thought that Nathan and Kai had been a part of the same military program.

When she finished, she leaned back in her chair, grabbed her water to take another sip, and then waited to hear their reaction.

Had she come this far only for Kai and Gage to continue denying what she said? Or would Kai own up to the truth?

Because she knew in her gut that she was on the right track, even if he wouldn't admit it.

CHAPTER
SIX

WHEN TORI FINISHED, Kai's thoughts continued to race.

She hadn't changed any details—a good indicator she was telling the truth.

But if this was the truth, then he and Gage were in trouble.

Kai thanked her for sharing. Then he glanced at Gage. "Can you and I talk outside?"

"Sure."

Before they exited the room, Kai turned back to Tori. "Deadbolt the door behind us, and don't answer for anyone but me or Gage. Understand?"

Her eyes widened with a flash of fear before she nodded. "I understand."

He and Gage stepped out of the room and walked

to the end of the hallway, where they would have a little more privacy.

Then Kai crossed his arms and turned to his colleague. "What do you think?"

Gage rubbed his chin, looking just as unsettled as Kai felt. "I don't know. She sounds legit."

"But if she's telling the truth, then who is this Nathan guy? I've never heard of him before. He didn't come through the program with us."

"I have no idea, and I helped train everyone who's come through Project Elevate."

"Could there be another secret program?" Kai asked. "Another set of recruits?"

Gage twisted his neck skeptically. "I find that hard to believe. Then again, I *shouldn't* find it hard to believe. There are so many secrets and so much classified information involved with what we do . . . I'm sure there's a lot we're in the dark about."

"Larchmont would know."

"But he won't tell us."

Kai paused, unsure if he should say this next part. But he had to. Skirting around the truth would do no one any good. "What if Larchmont sent these guys after Tori?"

He and Gage stared at each other.

Neither of them wanted to admit that Kai's words could be a reality. But they both knew the scenario was worth considering. Larchmont was slippery. Kai still wasn't sure he could truly trust the man.

Larchmont claimed to be looking out for the best interests of his men, but Kai often wondered if his boss was only looking out for his own interests.

The man was controlling, and oftentimes he had a good reason for it. But that didn't mean he was always right or that his intentions were always pure.

"If what you said is correct," Gage started, his words coming slowly, thoughtfully, "and if Larchmont sent these guys after Tori because she found out too much information, then he'll also know you're with her. Maybe even that I'm with her."

Kai's gut tightened.

He knew what Larchmont was capable of. The man got things done—and he didn't bat an eye at who was affected by his missions. People weren't important to him. Getting what he wanted was.

Kai crossed his arms. Usually, he knew exactly what to do in these situations. But when it came to possibly betraying the organization and/or man who'd made Kai into who he was, he needed to be sure his actions were wise and not a knee-jerk reaction.

Emotions didn't usually cloud his judgment, but right now his sense of betrayal had kicked in. Feelings about his past were surfacing. Memories of being given up by his family. Of having no one he could depend on.

A pang of emptiness echoed inside him at the thoughts.

"What should we do?" he asked Gage.

"I don't think we have any choice but to find out exactly what's going on here. Not only for Tori's sake, but for our sakes as well."

Kai couldn't help but agree.

———

Tori tried to drink the rest of her water, but nausea roiled inside her.

Every sip of liquid that went into her stomach ended up churning until she felt as if she might throw up. That was the last thing she wanted. She already had enough problems.

Kai and his colleague talked somewhere down the hallway. She knew that the outcome of that conversation would dictate what happened next.

Even though Kai had helped her thus far, it was still possible for him to change his mind and walk away.

Maybe being amenable to her was just a flash-in-the-pan reaction, and he was done.

Questions continued to stir inside her, leaving her lightheaded.

Finally, a knock sounded at the door. "Tori, it's me. Kai. Open up."

She peered through the peephole first to make sure it was him—just as she'd been directed. Sure enough, Kai stood on the other side.

Quickly, she unlocked the deadbolt and let both Kai and Gage inside.

They all gravitated back toward the table and sat around it, Gage and Tori in the two chairs and Kai on the corner of the bed across from them.

Her stomach continued to churn as she waited to hear their decision.

What if they said no? What would she do then?

Could she even find answers on her own? Or would those men track her down first? What would they do then? Kill her?

She hadn't considered these questions when she'd left her home in Florida this morning. She figured she'd simply have a conversation with Kai. Get some answers.

That she'd go from there.

Things had escalated so quickly.

She wiped her sweaty palms on her jeans as she waited, the seconds ticking by slower than a broken IV drip.

"We're going to help you," Kai finally announced.

Relief swept through her. "Thank you."

"But we have some questions for you first."

Gage's gaze looked intense as he studied her. "How close were you and your brother?"

"Even though he was eight years older, we were pretty close." Tori leaned back in her seat, trying to ease the tension between her shoulders. "However, we didn't reconnect until later in life."

Kai tilted his head. "What do you mean?"

"Our parents were killed in a motorcycle accident when we were younger," she explained. "We didn't have any other relatives, so Nathan and I were placed into two different foster care families when we were young. We lost touch for a long time. But when I turned twenty-one, I decided I wanted to look for him. I was able to trace him back to his foster parents from high school, who told me Nathan had joined the military. So then I went through the process of tracking him down there. Once we reconnected, it was like we'd never been apart. We talked all the time."

Kai and Gage exchanged a look that made her uncomfortable—one full of unspoken conversations she wasn't privy to.

What did they know that she didn't?

They exchanged another look before Kai shifted. "The program we were part of . . ."

Her breath caught. He'd just admitted they were part of a program.

At least she'd gotten that answer.

"We were chosen because we were unconnected," Kai continued. "That fact made it easier for us to give our entire lives to the program. None of us had anyone holding us back."

Tori let those words wash over her. She supposed they made sense.

Nathan would have fit that profile—at surface level, at least. The two of them met up once or twice a year, but otherwise they both did their own thing. On paper . . . it wouldn't appear they were close.

However, there had been a couple of occasions when odd things had arisen that had prevented them from seeing each other. Last minute canceled flights. Vague texts that didn't clarify details. Mysteriously canceled reservations on trips.

Could that have been because someone hadn't wanted them to see each other—someone with the power to manipulate those things?

She couldn't be sure.

"Did Nathan try to find you when he turned eighteen?" Kai asked. "He could have adopted you."

Tori shook her head. "No. He told me once that he came to visit me. When he got to the house, he saw me playing in the backyard. He said I looked happy, and that he knew if he took me away, my life would only be more complicated. He thought he was doing me a favor when he walked away."

The memory still caused a lump to form in her

throat. How she wished things had been different. That Nathan had talked to her that day.

Because things weren't as happy as they'd looked. She would have much rather been with Nathan.

"Where did Nathan live?" Gage asked.

"Georgia," she told them. "Near Athens."

Kai nodded slowly. "Tomorrow, we're going to head down there. For now, we'll grab some pizza for dinner, gather whatever clothing or toiletries we might need, and prepare for the trip. Meanwhile, we keep our heads down. We need to stay off these guys' radar. If they find us again, all they're going to do is slow us up."

Tori could think of much worse things those men might do.

But either way, she hoped they'd lost the men for good. Yet she didn't dare let herself believe that.

KAI, Gage, and Tori awoke before the sun rose to make the ten-hour drive to Georgia.

They'd grabbed some food—powdered donuts, a cinnamon roll, and some mini muffins—from the vending machines downstairs. They weren't the healthiest options, but Kai figured they would work for now.

Then they climbed into Gage's SUV and left.

Tori sat in the back seat. An hour into the trip, her head was against the door and her eyes closed.

Kai knew she'd tossed and turned last night. He'd taken first watch near the door while Gage had gotten some shut-eye in the adjoining room.

Her thoughts were clearly haunting her. He couldn't blame her. Who wouldn't feel like that in these circumstances? All things considered, Tori was handling the situation exceedingly well.

When Kai was certain Tori was asleep, he turned to Gage and quietly asked, "You heard from Larchmont?"

The man liked to check in. Going radio silent would only raise suspicions.

Gage rubbed his jaw and nodded. "He checked in with me last night. I had no choice but to answer his call since I'm supposed to be on assignment."

Kai figured as much.

He frowned. He had a love-hate relationship with the man. On one hand, Larchmont had made him into the person he was today. He'd given Kai opportunities. Had believed in him and become a father figure.

Father figures didn't always have a good connotation for Kai, though, especially given his past.

"Did Larchmont ask any questions or sound suspicious?" Kai asked.

"He asked for an update." Gage still gripped the wheel, his gaze fixated outside where the mid-September sun rose in the otherwise clear blue sky. "I told him I needed to go dark for a while but would be in touch soon."

"Did he ask why?"

"I told him it was something personal I needed to take care of."

"Did he buy it?" Kai asked.

"I think so." Gage stared at the road ahead. "It's hard to say with Larchmont."

"Knowing him, he's probably suspicious." Kai let out a sigh.

"He's always been a micromanager."

That would be an understatement.

Kai glanced behind him again to confirm Tori was still sleeping.

She looked so innocent as she rested. Her dark hair fell in soft waves around her face and shoulders. Her milky skin was smooth and unblemished and her lips full. When awake, her eyes were big and bright.

Tori was unlike most of the people he encountered. He usually thought the worst of strangers and people he met on assignment. But not Tori. She was just as much a victim as her brother might have been.

Kai thought about what she'd told him yesterday, about how she'd grown up in the foster care system. So had he, and he knew what a tough place it could be—especially for a female. They were so much more vulnerable.

He hated the thought of it—that anyone had to go through the system, really. But when adults couldn't act or behave like adults, that was what happened.

Despite that, her story left him feeling unsettled. No operative trained through Project Elevate would share that kind of information. They'd been taught to keep those details private—at all costs.

It wasn't just a matter of their own safety. It was a matter of the well-being of those around them also. If the wrong people discovered who they really were and some of the missions they'd been on, then their lives would be on the line.

So they stayed quiet. Said they were former military and current security agents that mostly did bodyguard work.

However, no other operative had close family members either. Maybe that was why Nathan had decided to share those details with his sister. And if he'd had a crisis of conscience or thought his life was in danger . . .

Kai frowned.

There was still a lot more he needed to figure out.

———

When Tori awoke, it was quiet in the SUV.

She straightened and glanced out the window. The sun had risen high in the sky.

Based on the rolling hills around them, they could be . . . anywhere. But if she had to guess, they were in the North Carolina foothills.

She wasn't sure how long she'd been asleep, but

the rest had been nice. She'd been tired lately. She hadn't slept well—not since her brother died, and she'd seen the autopsy report. When she'd begun questioning what happened, she'd really thrown herself into an emotional tailspin.

"Good afternoon," Kai said from the front seat.

"Afternoon?" Had she slept that long? She must have needed the rest.

"It's just barely past noon," Kai said. "We're going to stop in a minute for a bathroom break and to grab some lunch at a fast-food place. We'll run inside, pay with cash for our food, and then eat in the car. It's the smartest thing we can do."

Tori nodded in agreement and sat up a little straighter. She wiped her chin, hoping she hadn't drooled or done anything else embarrassing. "That sounds good."

Now that Kai mentioned it, she could use a quick break. Her body felt stiff.

A few minutes later, they pulled into a burger joint, and Gage parked. Kai walked beside her as she headed for the bathroom. Just as earlier, Tori noticed how he constantly looked around, as if checking to make sure they weren't being followed.

She deeply appreciated that quality about him. It made her feel safe.

Kind of like being around Nathan had made her

feel safe. He, too, would keep a watchful eye out for any possible dangers. And when she'd been dating Michael, Nathan immediately hadn't liked the man. If Michael had ever talked down to her, Nathan had quickly put the man in his place.

Nathan had clearly seen the truth about Michael's character before Tori had. If only she'd listened to her brother, she could have saved herself a lot of heartbreak.

What kind of training program had these guys gone through that had made them so sharp? That had made their reflexes so quick and their instincts so refined?

Fifteen minutes later, Tori had a chicken sandwich, a side of fruit, and unsweetened tea. It was the healthiest thing she could find on the menu.

She settled in the back seat for the rest of the drive.

As she took the first bite of her sandwich, she realized her appetite wasn't as strong as she thought. In fact, every bite made her feel sick to her stomach—something she couldn't afford to feel during such a long trip.

She set the rest of her food aside, telling herself she'd eat it later once her stomach felt more settled.

Kai glanced back at her. "How did you say your brother died again?"

"Cardiac arrest." Her voice grew soft. "He'd just

had a physical, and the doctor had said Nathan was healthy. It all seemed suspicious to me. But, as a nurse, I know sometimes these horrible things can happen, seemingly out of nowhere. I probably wouldn't have thought that much of it, except . . ."

"Except what?" Kai asked.

She hesitated a moment before responding. "There were things about Nathan that concerned me. He got bad headaches sometimes. Had some heart palpitations. He'd forget everyday things that he shouldn't have had trouble remembering like the name of the street where he lived."

"Is that right?" Kai's throat tightened.

"At first, I feared he might have a brain tumor, and I insisted he go see a friend of mine who's a doctor."

"When was that?" Kai asked.

"Six months ago. He always went to see military doctors before that."

"What did your friend say?"

"He looked at all the results and the bloodwork and the X-rays and said Nathan was fine, that all the test results were normal. He said maybe it was the tension of Nathan's job that was causing these 'episodes.'"

"It sounds like you were being thorough," Gage said.

"After Nathan died, I requested to see the

autopsy results." Tori paused and rubbed her throat. "Usually, it can take more than a month to get the results back. They got these results back to me in a week. I couldn't believe it, especially since I asked the detective for extra blood tests. All normal. Honestly . . . I think the coroner's findings were altered. They labeled his death as from natural causes. I just don't buy it."

"So you think someone messed with the autopsy results in order not to raise any red flags?" Kai turned his head toward her as if wanting to see her reaction.

Tori hesitated before nodding. "That's exactly what I think. Either the coroner fudged the report, or someone else altered the results after the fact."

Kai grunted.

"Did Nathan tell you much about the program?" Gage stole a glance at her in the rearview mirror before grabbing some french fries and taking a bite.

"Enough to make me uncomfortable. I begged him to get out. But he said it wasn't that easy."

Based on the silence of the two men in the front seat, she would guess they agreed with that statement.

"Why would someone want to kill him, and who could this person be?" Kai asked.

Those questions were something Tori had thought a lot about. She'd only come to one conclusion. "I think Nathan was asking too many questions and made someone nervous. I also think he lost his life in order to keep him quiet."

"What set these questions in motion?"

"He was really bummed a few months ago after his friend died in a car accident," she said. "I believe that led to him asking questions."

"What else do you know?"

She blew out a breath. "From what I understand, Vintage—that's the name his friend who died went by—had begun to experience some terrible headaches. He wasn't satisfied with the answers he was getting. He decided to look into things on his own."

"And?"

"He set the ball in motion, so to speak. He tracked down some names and addresses. But before he could truly discover anything, he died. My brother didn't like that."

Silence stretched.

Finally, Kai asked, "Did you go to anyone else with your concerns?"

"There was no one else I thought would believe me—or that I trusted with the information. I felt lost and confused, and I didn't know who to go to. Except you."

"So how do you think Nathan found my name and address?" Kai asked.

"I believe his friend tracked down your information, and Nathan went up to DC to check things out. I'm not sure why he didn't end up talking to you."

"I've been traveling some," he said.

"Then maybe that was why. But I know he listed your name. It even had a star beside it. Like I said, that's why I came to DC. To find you. I was trying to get a feel for you before I approached to ask for help. But then you saw me and . . ." Her voice trailed.

She didn't like that memory. Didn't like the flashback of her face being pressed into that brick wall. Of her hands being pinned behind her back. Of being worried that Kai might kill her.

Now that Tori had been around him longer, she'd seen a kinder side of him. She knew he'd just been reacting to her out of distrust. But if Kai had been through the same program Nathan had, then he was fully capable of killing her.

"I wasn't sure who you worked for," Kai explained again. "I'm sorry for being rough."

Her cheek still stung, and her wrists felt tender. But she kept that quiet. Those things were the least of her concerns right now.

"Which tells me you know all this secret military stuff is true, right?" Tori's throat burned as she asked the question.

Kai and Gage exchanged a glance with each other as she waited for an answer.

Would they continue to avoid her questions? Or would they finally confess to the truth?

Either way, Tori had no choice but to trust them right now. She was at their mercy, a choice she prayed she didn't regret.

KAI'S JAW TIGHTENED. How much should he say?

Last night, after Tori had gone to bed, he'd done a thorough background check on her.

Her story checked out.

She really had been in foster care. Really was related to Nathan. Really was a traveling nurse based out of Florida.

He'd also discovered that she was single with no children. How much of her current lifestyle was because of her background, and how much was simply because she hadn't found the right person?

Or maybe Tori didn't want to marry or have kids. There were myriad reasons someone like her might want to remain unattached.

Just like Kai had his own reasons.

She hadn't given him any cause so far not to trust her. But in his line of work, he had to be careful. Opening up to the wrong person could be deadly—not only for him. He could also put his colleagues at risk—colleagues that were like brothers to him.

"The truth is, I've been asking a lot of questions myself lately," Kai finally said. "What your brother sent you is accurate."

He glanced back in time to see Tori's eyes widen.

"You *were* a part of the program then?" The words rushed out. "Gage too?"

"Yes," Gage answered.

Kai figured the fewer the details he shared the better. Gage was clearly on the same wave-length.

"Who is Larchmont?" she continued.

"He started as the commander in charge of what was known as Project Elevate," Kai said. "Project Elevate sounds similar to the program your brother went through. When Larchmont retired, he took several of us with him so he could start the Shadow Agency."

"And what is the Shadow Agency?"

"We do jobs that other people can't." Gage continued down the Interstate, zipping past other cars as they settled in for the long trip. "Jobs that require us to slip in and out, almost like ghosts. If we're caught . . . well, the truth is, we don't really exist on paper. The government can claim no association with us if needed."

Tori nodded slowly. "Where exactly can I find this Larchmont guy? I'd really like to talk to him."

"He's everywhere," Kai said.

She tilted her head. "What does that mean?"

"I guess you could say he's a man of mystery," Kai told her. "He's all over the place, and we never really know when he'll show up. He has a home in Wyoming, though I would never go assuming he'd be there."

She paused before asking, "Is what my brother said about Larchmont true? Could he have some knowledge of what's going on?"

Kai clenched his jaw again, unsure how to answer.

Yes, he'd had some suspicions lately. Suspicions he hadn't really pursued.

But since the man had been like a father figure to him, Kai didn't want to betray him unless he was certain the man had done something wrong.

Tori waited for his answer.

Finally, Kai licked his lips and said, "Possibly. We need to dig deeper until we can find answers."

———

They arrived in Georgia close to dinnertime.

But instead of getting something to eat, Kai wanted to head straight to Nathan's house.

Tori was relieved. She was eager to get there also.

The urgency pressing on her didn't allow room for anything else, only answers.

When she'd first started looking into her brother's death, that feeling wasn't present. But now, it was clear that someone was trying to hurt her—if not kill her—in order to stop her from finding out the truth.

If she didn't move quickly, these people might get their way.

But even when she discovered the truth . . . what would she do then?

She was a traveling nurse. She was powerless to do anything to stop people with the kind of money, resources, and influence involved here.

But she'd figure something out. She had to. For Nathan.

As they headed toward her brother's house, her anxiety grew. She hadn't been there since right after his funeral. She still hadn't decided whether or not to sell it. But she wasn't sure what to do with the place either. It wasn't as if she wanted to move here. But keeping the place up and paying taxes would quickly get old.

They pulled to a stop in front of the small, white house located in an older but neat neighborhood. A pang of grief hit Tori at the sight of it.

Her brother had been so proud when he'd bought this place. He'd even invited her up for the weekend to see it.

Right now, the grass was overgrown, and the flowerbeds needed to be weeded. All things Tori would have to think about later. She wasn't ready to sell it yet. In the meantime, she would need to take care of it.

It was what Nathan would have wanted.

As the SUV rolled to a stop, Kai turned back to her. "You ready for this?"

Tori drew in a deep breath as she tried to calm her racing heart. "As ready as I'll ever be."

KAI AND GAGE had decided that Gage would remain at the door while Kai went inside Nathan's place with Tori.

Kai hadn't seen anyone following them on the way here. That meant no one should know where they were. Still, they needed to take every precaution possible, especially since they didn't know what or who they were up against. Larchmont? Maybe. Or it could be an enemy they didn't even know existed?

Tori unlocked the door, and they stepped inside.

A tidy house stared back at them, one with hardwood floors, beige furniture, and a black entertainment center with an oversized TV.

Standard bachelor pad—except for how clean it was. He wondered if Tori had cleaned it or if Nathan was always this organized.

If Nathan had gone through the same training as Kai, then Kai would guess this place was always this clean.

Kai quickly scanned the rooms and noticed the lack of personal decorations. Was that because Nathan was a typical guy who didn't care about decorating? Or was it because, as part of Project Elevate, they'd learned to keep things as impersonal as possible?

There were no pictures. No mementos from trips. No trophies from childhood or from community softball teams. Not even any mugs from their favorite coffeehouses.

The lack of anything personal was in preparation for always being ready. If an enemy was looking for them, they shouldn't leave anything behind that could indicate who they were or where they might be. There would be no trail of their favorite places.

When there wasn't much evidence, things were easier to erase and disappear.

Kai himself had just rented an apartment in DC. The District of Columbia wasn't his top choice of places to live, but Larchmont needed someone to act as a point man for the region. Kai had been tasked with the job.

He'd gone from one lonely existence to another. He told himself it was better that way. But this move had felt tough, further cementing his future.

His next-door neighbors were a family with two small children. As he listened to them—the walls were thinner than he would have liked—he often felt a twinge of regret. Maybe even jealousy.

Tori stepped farther inside, running her hand across the kitchen counter with a far-off expression on her face. Then she paused near a bookshelf, her back toward him.

Was she looking for something among the books there?

He stepped closer to see for himself.

When he did, he noticed the moisture glimmering in her gaze.

Compassion clutched his heart.

Kai hadn't even thought about how hard this visit might be on her. Nathan had only been dead for a couple of weeks. Her grief was still fresh.

He reached for her shoulder and squeezed. "I'm sorry . . ."

She didn't make any eye contact as she nodded. "I hoped for more time with him, you know? I wanted the two of us to be able to hang out more. I imagined us having families of our own one day and going on vacation together. Spending holidays crammed into this small house but loving every minute of being together. I always thought that it would happen one day . . . but sometimes one day never comes."

Kai felt an unusual well of emotions. He longed

for the same things. Except he always pushed down those desires and reminded himself that those things weren't his lot in life.

He didn't say anything, though. He let her finish instead.

"I figured it was okay to be single as long as I had people in my life—as long as I had family. Then I wouldn't be so alone." Tori's voice cracked. "Yet here I am . . ."

A lump formed in Kai's throat, but he swallowed it. He understood those sentiments all too well. He'd been thinking entirely too much about his past and his future lately.

Maybe it was his age. He'd recently turned thirty. Sometimes, he just wanted to put down roots.

"I get that," he finally said. He squeezed her shoulder again before dropping his hand. "I would love to be able to stand here with you longer and reminisce. But we should probably look for anything you might have missed."

"Of course."

She began rifling through the bookshelves. While she did that, Kai looked through the kitchen cabinets and drawers.

Nothing caught his eye.

If Nathan had been with Project Elevate, he would have known not to keep anything at home.

Kai wasn't sure what he expected to find here. But they at least had to check it out, just in case.

"I'll search his bedroom," Tori said.

Kai followed her down the hallway and into the bedroom. While she looked in his dresser, he searched under the bed and in the vents.

Still nothing.

Had they come all this way for no reason?

"Guys," Gage called from the doorway. "The same car has driven by twice. I don't like it."

Kai's shoulders tightened. "We need to get out of here."

"Already?" Tori's voice lilted with fear. "Do you think those guys found us?"

"Doesn't matter," Kai grabbed her arm. "We can't take the chance."

———

A tremble rushed through Tori.

Could those men be here? The ones who'd followed her yesterday?

Or maybe there was a whole network of other people. She really knew so little about what was going on.

"Come on." Kai pulled her toward the door.

She could hardly catch her breath as she anticipated what might happen next.

"We get to the car, and you stay low, understand?" Kai rushed.

"Understood." But her voice sounded shaky.

Gage pulled out his gun as they stepped onto the porch. He held up a hand, indicating they should stay back.

Then, still scanning the street, he stepped from the porch toward the car.

Before he cleared the steps, a black sedan squealed to a stop in front of them.

Bullets flew through the air.

"Watch out!" Kai instinctively shielded Tori with his own body as they dove back inside.

"Get out of here!" Gage yelled from his position behind a brick column on the porch.

More gunshots sounded.

Tori's heart stuttered in her ears. Was Gage okay?

Kai didn't stop to find out. He helped her to her feet and then pulled her toward the back of the house.

"But Gage . . ." Tori murmured, worried about the man.

"He knows how to take care of himself," Kai yelled. "He'll catch up."

Before she could argue anymore, they flew out the back door and across the lawn.

"Remember when I helped you scale that fence yesterday?" Kai called over his shoulder.

"Can't forget it."

"Good. Because we're going to do it again. Keep your eyes open for any dogs."

"What?" Tori asked breathlessly.

Before she could think about it more, Kai boosted her over the fence. She landed with a roll on the grass on the other side. Thankfully, this fence was shorter than the one yesterday. Still, her hip ached when she'd hit the ground, a reminder of yesterday's mishaps.

Heart pounding in her ears, she glanced around.

She didn't see any dogs, only a swing set and a cute but empty brick patio.

Kai landed with a steady thump on the grass beside her. "We've got to keep moving. We have no time to waste."

He grabbed her hand again, and they cut through the backyard and out the gate.

When they reached the street, they didn't slow down or even attempt to look casual, despite the fact people were outside. One man was jogging. Another worked on his lawn.

Kai cut through the yard across the street and into another backyard.

They ran so fast and so far that Tori didn't even know where they were or where they were going. She simply held onto Kai and followed his instructions.

He seemed to know what he was doing—much more than Tori would know to do in a situation like this.

By the time they stopped on a sidewalk, she had to pause for a moment. She bent forward, hands on her knees, and tried to catch her breath.

"You good?" Kai observed her, hardly winded at all.

"I think so." She said the words through raspy breaths. "What about Gage?"

"He'll catch up with us." As Kai looked in the distance, his eyes widened.

She swerved her neck around to see what he was looking at—even though she was fairly certain she already knew.

It was the black sedan. Again.

Despite their desperation to get away, those gunmen had found them.

CHAPTER
TEN

KAI THREW Tori on the ground before throwing himself on top of her.

How had these guys found them so quickly?

Bullets shattered the air, and the scent of smoke hung like a cloud around them.

Sirens sounded in the distance. No doubt, the neighbors—at least one of them—had reported the gunfire.

Would the shooters flee?

Kai couldn't be certain.

The men fired off a few more shots.

As they did, a sharp, hot pain sliced through Kai's upper arm.

As he reached for it, the car squealed away.

Most likely, those guys were gone. But he couldn't

be certain. There was a chance the assailants would be back.

Either way, he needed to keep Tori safe.

He stood, ignoring the pain in his arm. Whatever had happened, he would be okay. His injury didn't hurt that bad.

The important thing was that he and Tori keep moving.

"This way!" Instead of running in the opposite direction of the car, they ran toward the area where the vehicle had just disappeared.

He liked this situation less and less, especially since this part of the neighborhood was more crowded. People jogged. Moms walked with strollers. A teen scrolled through her phone while walking her golden retriever.

If they'd heard the bullets flying, they must have assumed it was a car backfiring.

This wasn't just about keeping Tori safe. He didn't want any of these innocent bystanders to be hurt either.

They cut onto another street.

"Kai . . . you're bleeding," Tori said behind him.

He figured as much. One of the bullets had most likely skimmed his arm.

"I'm fine," he muttered.

Just as they turned another corner, the black sedan appeared on the street in front of them.

The vehicle would be upon them faster than they could run away.

Kai needed to figure out a plan, and he needed to figure it out now.

————

Tori saw the car, and all the air left her lungs.

What would they do now?

Just as that thought raced through her mind, another vehicle pulled up beside them.

A familiar SUV.

The window rolled down, and Gage appeared. "Get in. Now."

Kai shoved her inside before jumping into the vehicle himself. Before he even shut the door, Gage hit the accelerator.

"Buckle up. We've got to lose them." Gage gripped the wheel, but he didn't appear unnerved.

Which was the opposite of how Tori felt.

Another tremble raked through her.

Never in her life had she been so terrified.

She thought she could trust Kai and Gage and prayed she wasn't wrong.

She snapped her seatbelt in place as Gage continued to speed through the streets.

Thankfully, he'd managed to get back to the SUV and find them.

She didn't know how Gage knew where to look for them, but she was glad he did.

Tori had no doubt these two men were highly trained—just like Nathan had been.

When they'd been out to dinner together once, a man had tried to snatch her purse. In five seconds flat, Nathan had tripped the man, pinned him on the ground, and called the police.

She'd watched in amazement at his skills. His instincts had been truly remarkable.

But right now, she and Kai still weren't safe.

They had to lose these guys first.

How would they do that? It seemed like this game of chase would never end.

"Hold on!" Just then, Gage jerked the steering wheel so fast that Tori collided into the door.

He pulled into the driveway of a red-brick ranch house.

What was he doing?

He drove all the way up to the side of the house, under a carport, then cut the engine.

"Kai?" Her heart pounded in her ears as doubt filled her.

Was this a setup? Had Tori been wrong to trust him?

"Duck," he muttered.

She did as he instructed.

Kai and Gage also ducked.

Their plan hit her. They were trying to disappear, to blend in with the other cars in the neighborhood. If those gunmen who were following them weren't looking closely, they wouldn't realize that Gage had parked.

It was a brilliant plan, actually. If she weren't in fear for her life, she might just be impressed.

Tori squeezed her eyes closed and prayed that the strategy worked.

KAI FROZE AS HE WAITED.

Those guys should be coming by anytime now.

He hoped this risk paid off. If it didn't, he, Tori, and Gage would be sitting ducks.

He lifted his head just enough to see through the back glass. Thankfully, the vehicle had tinted windows. Anyone driving by shouldn't see them inside.

Mere seconds later, a black sedan zoomed past.

The driver didn't appear to be looking for them in any driveways. They must be assuming Kai, Gage, and Tori were still driving—just as Gage had wagered.

Kai let out a breath.

But it was too soon to relax. Their plan could still backfire.

They waited several more seconds before Gage backed out of the driveway and headed down the road in the opposite direction.

He'd definitely just bought them some time.

"What do we do now?" Tori's voice didn't sound as strong as it had earlier.

This incident had definitely shaken her.

"I reserved a safe house," Gage called over his shoulder.

"You can reserve a safe house?" Confusion marred her voice.

"It's a rental house, but I booked it using a different ID and a prepaid credit card," Gage explained. "No one should be able to trace us there. It will give us a place where we can get our thoughts together—for a little while, at least."

"How far away is it?" Kai asked.

"Only about twenty minutes."

Kai scanned the road behind them again, halfway expecting to see that black sedan appear at any minute.

But he didn't see it.

Maybe they really had lost those guys.

Kai had hoped that after going to Nathan's house they would have more answers.

But instead, he only had more questions and more confirmation of the danger surrounding all of them.

Tori's thoughts raced as they headed down the road away from Nathan's place.

That had been close back there. So close. *Too* close.

She still wasn't sure they were safe yet.

There was so much she wanted to say, to ask. But her thoughts seemed to clog in her throat. She was still trying to process everything, but it would take a while.

She wanted to know: Who were those men? Why did they want to kill her? How had they even found her? Were these people that Nathan had, at one time, trusted?

The questions jostled around inside her.

Finally, Gage pulled up to the house where they'd be staying.

The place was fairly nondescript and located in the country, down a gravel lane surrounded by a grassy field and only a few trees.

If anyone started their way, Kai or Gage would see them. There was nowhere for a car to hide here.

However, Gage did pull his SUV into the attached garage, then volunteered to check out the house before they all went inside.

As he disappeared through the door, Tori remained in the back seat, a welcome quiet stretching between her and Kai.

The past twenty-four hours had her on edge. She halfway expected more bad things to happen. For trouble to be waiting inside. For her opponents to have anticipated their next move.

"Don't forget to breathe," Kai murmured.

That was when she realized she'd been holding her breath.

She released it with a quick, airy chuckle, embarrassed that Kai had noticed. "Of course."

Gage popped his head out the door and motioned for them to come inside.

Tori and Kai hurried into the small country home. She bypassed the kitchen and dining room and paused in a cozy living room with dark-blue couches and plum-colored accessories.

All the shades were drawn, making her feel more secure.

"Once it gets dark outside, we'll need to keep the lights off unless we're in an interior room with no windows," Gage said as if reading her thoughts.

She knew what he was saying. They needed to keep their presence here a secret for as long as they could. It only made sense.

She glanced at Kai and flinched when she saw the blood staining the sage green fabric of his shirt. A bullet must have skimmed his arm.

Blood in general didn't usually cause a reaction in her. As a nurse, she saw blood all the time.

The reaction was from the reality of everything that had just happened.

The reality of how much danger they were in.

The reality of how close they'd come to being killed.

"Let me check that out." Tori nodded toward his wound.

Kai opened his mouth as if to protest.

She quickly added, "Please. I *am* a nurse."

Finally, he shut his mouth and nodded.

She searched the bathroom and kitchen cabinets for gloves, but she didn't find any. Instead, she scrubbed her hands and wrists with soap and hot water to cut down on the chance of infection.

Then she motioned for Kai to sit at one of the dining room chairs. He obliged.

"Can I turn on the light above us?" she asked.

"That should be fine," he told her.

She flipped a switch, and a soft glow filled the room.

Then Tori lowered herself into the chair beside Kai and carefully tugged up his sleeve.

The bullet had definitely skimmed his bicep. But the blood had already begun to coagulate.

"Looks like you could use some stitches," she told him.

"Let's skip the stitches and just use some bandages. I'm not afraid of a little scarring." He glanced at his wound as if it weren't a big deal.

No, a person in his position most likely wasn't afraid of blemishes.

Gage strode into the room, a small first aid kit in his hand. "Found this in one of the closets."

Tori thanked him.

He nodded and then continued pacing the house as if on guard.

Did he fear someone had followed them? Probably.

How long would they be safe here?

Tori had no idea. But if she had to guess, not long.

She checked out the contents of the first aid kit. Still no gloves. But she found some antiseptic and began to clean the wound.

Kai didn't flinch, even though Tori knew it had to sting.

After she cleaned the cut, she used some ointment to prevent infection. Then she found some butterfly bandages to put across it.

He remained quiet as she worked, as if contemplating their next moves.

When she finished, she leaned back and let out a breath. "That should be okay for now. But we'll need to keep an eye on it. We can't let the wound get infected."

"Understood." Kai rolled his sleeve down.

She raked a hand through her hair, realizing that bandaging his wound had been a nice distraction.

Now that it was over, she was left with only her thoughts again.

"What now?" she asked.

Kai turned toward her, his expression placid as if this was just another average day. "Right now, I'd like to review all the documents Nathan left for you. I need to see exactly how deeply your brother was into this."

Tori swallowed hard. She knew that was what they needed to do. But another part of her feared what they might find out.

However, she couldn't let that fear stop her from finding answers—because answers just might be the only thing that would ensure their safety. Answers, and God's protection.

TWELVE

WHILE GAGE RAN out to grab some dinner and a few supplies for them, Kai laid out all the documents Tori had brought with her in the crossbody bag. He spread them on the table in front of him.

As he did that, Tori found some coffee and brewed a pot. Even though it was getting late, they both needed some caffeine.

Kai stared at the papers. There weren't very many and most were handwritten.

But there were blueprints—though he wasn't sure what buildings they went with. There were medical reports—for more than one person, it appeared. Certain elements had been circled. Others had exclamation points beside them.

Then there was a timeline that went back at least fifteen years. It appeared to be a timeline of Nathan's life, if he had to guess. There was high school graduation listed, joining military, being recruited for the special program.

There was a list of names—only last names, however. Kai didn't recognize any of them. But symptoms were listed beside each name. Symptoms that included headaches, tremors, blackouts, dizzy spells, personality changes.

The final page was another list of names, this list with "Suspects" written at the top.

Larchmont was the first name, and there was a red star beside it.

Other names were Commander Ken Davis and Senator Griff Wagner. There was a notation that said: "Who is Rafferty really? What is he hiding?" Then there was "Alias: Ridge Rock."

What did that mean?

He recognized Senator Wagner's name. Commander Davis sounded vaguely familiar.

But he had no idea who Ridge Rock might be or Rafferty.

This was very interesting. But it only raised more questions.

He found it curious that most of Nathan's notes were handwritten. Yet he understood also. Most digital things could be traced, and Nathan had wanted to keep this information secure. Kai might do the same thing.

He imagined Nathan—a man he didn't know—writing these notes. Driving the papers to Tori's house. Finding she wasn't there but leaving the information inside her oven, where it would be safe.

If Kai had been in Nathan's shoes, he would have left his phone at home while he traveled so he wouldn't have been tracked—just in case.

He would have probably borrowed a car also.

Had Nathan also done those things?

Thinking about those details made Kai sound paranoid, and he knew that. But in his line of work, it wasn't paranoia.

It was survival.

As a valuable asset of the government, he knew the military wouldn't have been able to simply let him go and continue on with his life. Sure, his former leaders had made them believe they were free. That they had walked away.

But they hadn't. And they all knew that.

The question looming in his mind was: Was the military behind the efforts to potentially silence Nathan? Or had it been Larchmont? Or maybe it had been someone else entirely, someone they hadn't yet considered.

If Kai's theory was wrong, and Nathan hadn't been killed to stop him from asking questions, then there were other possibilities. If Nathan had been part of Project Elevate, then he'd no doubt made uncountable enemies through his line of work. Any of them could be guilty.

Looking at Nathan's notes right now, Kai could definitely see where it might be someone from Nathan's past.

He'd noted his symptoms—all of which Tori had mentioned already.

He listed his suspects—his former boss, former colleagues, enemies.

He wrote down his fears—that someone close to him might actually be trying to kill him.

He'd also included his medical records, which on the surface appeared clear.

As Tori placed a cup of coffee in front of him, Kai paused at the autopsy report. He took a long sip of his drink before diving into the report.

Tori sat in the chair beside him, pulling it close so she could see over his shoulder.

"I've reviewed that autopsy report at least a dozen times," she said. "And it's true that I'm not a doctor so there could be things I don't understand or that I missed. But I don't see any reason why Nathan would have gone into cardiac arrest."

"If his death wasn't natural, then what's your theory on how it happened?"

She pressed her lips together, the tension building inside her obvious. Then she swallowed hard before saying, "Call me crazy, but certain medications can mimic or even cause cardiac arrest. If someone got their hands on those drugs, they could figure out how to make that happen."

He stole a glance at her. "Wouldn't these medications show up in the autopsy report?"

Her fingers hugged her coffee mug, though the drink mostly remained untouched. "The medical examiner ran a toxicology report, but no traces of drugs turned up in the results."

"But you're still suspicious of that?" Kai continued to watch her expression.

"Yes, I am. Someone's not telling the truth somewhere, and I'm trying to figure out who."

He took another sip of his coffee. "Nathan did a good job tracking his symptoms, including the time, day, and frequency."

"He was on top of it, for sure." She leaned back, her hand sweeping over her mouth. "Like I told you before, he'd been having some strange episodes he tried to dismiss. He said something about feeling out of sorts lately, but he couldn't put his finger on what exactly was wrong. He had spans of time he couldn't remember. Headaches. Tremors. Times he didn't feel like himself."

Kai's jaw hardened.

He wasn't sure if he was ready to admit this yet or not.

He knew the implications of his words.

But the truth was, Kai had been experiencing those exact same symptoms lately.

———

Tori studied Kai's face.

He wasn't sharing something, was he? Whatever thought he had, he kept it private. But what if that thought could help her find answers? This was no time to keep secrets—especially if those secrets had to do with her brother.

Kai caught her staring and did a double take.

Her thoughts raced with questions she didn't want to ask. Yet still, there were answers she needed to know. Those answers right now were more important than making Kai uncomfortable.

She tilted her head as she observed him. "What aren't you telling me?"

"Nothing," Kai said a little too quickly.

"I don't believe you." Tori crossed her arms and leaned back farther in the chair, her thoughts still racing. "When was the last time you had an X-ray with a doctor other than the one your boss provides?"

He shrugged and shook his head. "I can't really say for sure. I haven't had any reason to have an X-ray. Where are you going with this?"

She nibbled on her bottom lip as she contemplated how to word her next statement. "My theory about Nathan being administered medication that caused his heart to stop isn't my only suspicion. I've also wondered if some type of pacemaker was implanted inside Nathan. Pacemakers can be remotely monitored and controlled."

His forehead wrinkled. "Wouldn't that have shown up in the autopsy?"

"Yes. But not if someone was trying to cover something up."

Kai shifted, his gaze suddenly darkening. "What exactly are you implying?"

"I'm saying that if my brother didn't die of natural causes and he wasn't poisoned, then there's only one other reason I can think of he might have gone into cardiac arrest."

"And you think that reason is a pacemaker?"

"Or something similar—some type of device inside him that could have stopped his heart. I even wonder if maybe everyone who'd been in the program might have this device."

"I think if I'd had a pacemaker inserted, I would remember it," Kai started, a challenging look in his gaze. "Don't the batteries have to be changed every so often?"

"Yes, usually every five to eight years, and there would usually be a scar of some sort."

A few seconds of silence stretched.

Then Tori asked, "Could I see your chest please?"

Kai swallowed hard but nodded. "Why not?"

He pulled off his shirt, and Tori felt her throat go dry. But she remained professional. No way would she let her expression show just how impressive his defined muscles were.

Instead, her gaze went to the area of his chest near his heart where a pacemaker would have been implanted.

She ran her fingers over his skin. Then she squinted and leaned closer. "Is that a scar?"

He shrugged. "I was injured by some shrapnel. Had to get stitches."

She pulled her gaze from his chest to his eyes. "Are you sure?"

"Sure that shrapnel hit me?" He squinted. "I remember it clearly."

A car rumbled down the lane. She checked and saw it was Gage. A moment later, the garage door opened.

"You're sure that's where this scar is from?" Tori asked Kai.

"What else could it be?"

She touched it again, squinting to examine it closer.

Just then, Gage walked into the room with a pizza in hand and made a face. "I hope I'm not interrupting something."

"No, of course not." Tori cleared her throat and stepped back. "Strange request, but could I see your chest?"

Gage glanced at Kai, who shrugged.

Gage didn't ask any questions. Instead, he put the pizza on the table and took his shirt off.

Tori examined his chest. "You have a mark too."

He glanced down and touched the faint line. Just like Kai, the mark was barely visible. But the scar was definitely there. Usually, she would see a lump also, but not this time.

She couldn't explain that—unless the device had been planted somewhere else in his body.

"I got that when we were on a mission in Uzbekistan," Gage said. "You should see the other guy."

Tori barely registered his attempt at being light-hearted. "Then why do you guys have the exact same mark? In the exact same location?"

The two of them exchanged a glance. But they said nothing.

Tori knew why.

Because there was nothing they could say that fit the narrative they'd been taught to believe.

KAI'S MUSCLES tensed as he processed what Tori had just told him. The thought of him having a pacemaker implanted without giving permission or being made aware of the device inside his body left him unsettled.

It wasn't a feeling he experienced often.

He tugged his shirt back on. So did Gage.

"So let's say your theory is correct." He shifted and crossed his arms as he stared at Tori. The pizza was getting cold, but he didn't care. "How would I prove that it's true?"

"You would go in for a test—an X-ray," she explained. "It would show if you had any devices in your body. Is that what you want to do?"

Kai glanced at his colleague. "I don't know about

you, but now that the thought is in my head, I have to know."

"If she's right, then what happened to Nathan could happen to us," Gage said. "To any of us. Even Austin, and he's a dad now."

The implications of the situation washed over Kai yet again.

He met Tori's gaze. "Your doctor friend, the one who looked at your brother . . . where is he located?"

"His name is Landon Jean-Pierre, and he's in Atlanta," she told him. "The two of us went to medical school together."

"I didn't think nurses went to medical school." A wrinkle of confusion formed on Kai's brow.

He wanted to trust Tori, but he had to be cautious. He couldn't afford to trust the wrong person, and something about her story didn't add up in his mind.

"We don't." She swallowed hard. "I started medical school with plans of becoming a doctor. But I had to drop out. I became a nurse instead."

Kai nodded slowly. There was more to her story. He was certain of it.

What could have happened to make her quit?

When she didn't explain any further, he didn't ask. Maybe she'd open up later.

"I say we go visit this doctor tomorrow," Kai said. "We need answers. If your brother's medical tests all came back clear, then something is wrong.

Someone is lying or covering up something. Your friend might have those answers. Now we need those answers, not only about Nathan but about ourselves too."

"Let's do it." Gage grabbed two pieces of pizza and then pointed down the hallway. "Now, if you don't mind, I'm going to go call Nia and see how she's doing. She had a big meeting today. Don't worry—my phone is new and untraceable."

Nia, Gage's girlfriend, lived and ran a company down in Miami. The two had met a few months ago, and she'd originally been Gage's number one suspect in the murder of his friend. Together, they'd found the real killer, and they'd been seeing each other since then.

Kai was happy for his friend. He'd watched the two of them work things out long-distance. Gage seemed really happy and hopeful about his future with Nia—despite his past.

Would Kai ever get to that point? He wasn't sure.

Tomorrow, Kai hoped to have some answers. But he had to wonder if he became too much of a threat if he might drop dead at any minute also.

He could try to protect himself from bullets and oncoming cars and all sorts of other dangers.

But if someone had implanted a device in his chest, there was no way he could protect himself from the outcome of that.

In the meantime, he grabbed a piece of pizza also. He'd need food if he wanted to keep his energy up.

————

Tori knew she should try to sleep.

But she couldn't. Though she was physically tired, her mind still raced.

Kai didn't seem in a hurry to go to bed either. While Gage jumped in the shower, they both glanced at each other while munching on their dinner.

"Did you take off work for a while?" Kai asked.

She nodded. "I took a leave of absence after my brother's death. Then I found the package he left me. I knew I couldn't let that go. I had to find answers before I could even think about going back to my job. So I decided to find you first."

"That's respectable."

"What about you?" She tilted her head. "Did I pull you away from any cases?"

"I'm actually in between assignments right now as I try to get a satellite office in DC established."

"Why you? Why did you get picked to set up this office?" Tori was genuinely curious.

"My boss found that one of my gifts was administration. I agree with that. So I said yes. I thought some stability might be good for me."

"Because you traveled a lot?"

"I went where the job took me." He paused. "Did your brother do the same after he got out of the military? I never asked you what exactly he did for a living."

"He said he worked for a government contractor. But he never really told me specifics, just that he was using the skills he'd learned while in the military. I figured he was doing some kind of security."

"Name of his company?"

"He never said, and I never asked." She frowned. "It didn't seem important."

"What about at the funeral? Didn't he have a boss or coworker who showed up?"

Her frown deepened. "He didn't want a funeral. So I took his ashes and spread them over a mountain. I did get a card from the Blackstone Company, signed by some coworkers. But that's all."

"No records of his paychecks?" Kai asked.

"No. I'm not sure if they paid him in cash or what. But I couldn't find anything. I even tried to connect his health insurance with an employer, but apparently he didn't have health insurance. I found that hard to believe."

"Interesting," Kai murmured. "Anything else?"

She let out a breath. "Nathan did travel quite a bit. Never had any serious relationships. Was more of a lone ranger."

"Sounds about right . . ." A frown tugged at his lips before disappearing.

Tori studied his face, curious about the man in front of her. "What's your background? You know a little about me. I virtually know nothing about you."

He let out a long breath, almost as if he was trying to think of a way to avoid answering her question. But it was just the two of them, no interruptions. He had no excuses.

"I grew up in California," he started. "My mom . . . well, she was a druggie. She died of an overdose when I was eight. I was then sent to live with my dad in Hawaii."

"Hawaii is nice . . ."

"I'm sure it is. Only, he didn't really want me. I didn't understand why, so I made up excuses in my mind—usually blaming it on his work schedule or his new wife being too demanding. Whatever the truth was, he sent me back to California to live with my mother's brother."

"I'm sorry," Tori murmured. "That had to be hard."

His face showed very little emotion. "That didn't really work out either. By that point, I had started to rebel. I acted out in school. Snuck out of the house at night. Did thrill-seeking type of activities. I was tired of being passed around and feeling like a nobody, I guess. By the time I was twelve, my uncle gave up custody, and I went to live in a children's home. Eventually, I was placed with a foster family. Then another and another. I never stayed with any of them for long."

Her heart panged with grief. "I know what that's like."

"As soon as I graduated from high school, I needed something to do, a way to support myself. I was suddenly on my own. So I joined the military."

"It sounds like a tough life, but you've done well for yourself." Tori meant the words.

Kai seemed smart and respectable. He treated people well—if Tori didn't count the first day they'd met when he thought she was an enemy.

"I've always thanked Larchmont for whipping me into shape," Kai said. "Now that's all in question."

Her lips pressed together in a frown. "I can only imagine how difficult that must be."

She wanted to ask more. To reach out and touch him.

But she wasn't sure those things would be wise. They didn't know each other that well. He seemed standoffish. Touching him seemed like it would be crossing a line.

"That woman in the Vietnamese restaurant . . . how did you know her?" The question sounded unimportant, but she was genuinely curious.

"I like to eat there after work sometimes. And

since I speak the language, she decided she likes me. Hanh is a nice woman."

His words showed Tori a different side of him . . . a warmer, more personal side.

A side she liked more than the guy who'd manhandled her when they'd first met.

The bathroom door opened, and Gage stepped out, hair wet from his shower. Tori knew the interruption was probably a good thing.

Maybe she and Kai understood each other a little too well.

There weren't many people she could say that about.

And she wasn't sure how it made her feel. Most days she didn't want anyone to understand how much pain she'd felt while growing up.

CHAPTER
FOURTEEN

TORI HARDLY SLEPT ALL NIGHT. She halfway expected one of those men to show up at the house, guns blazing, determined to silence her—just like they'd silenced Nathan. Only they hadn't used guns to silence him. But the idea was the same: desperate men doing desperate things.

However, all had been quiet.

In the morning, she climbed out of bed and quietly crept into the bathroom to shower. The hot water felt good as it pounded her skin and relaxed her muscles. If only it could wash away all her worries.

Afterward, she dressed in some black leggings and a slouch gray top Gage had picked up. He'd run to the store last night to buy them clothes and food to hold them over.

These would work. Meanwhile, she'd washed the clothes she'd worn yesterday so she could wear them again. As far as the clothes she'd left at the other hotel when she'd first arrived in DC . . . maybe Tori could retrieve her bag when this was all over.

When she left the bathroom, she found Gage and Kai sitting at the dining room table with a box of donuts in front of them.

Seeing Kai sitting at the table with his dark hair freshly washed and his face clean-shaven did something strange to her heart. It let out an involuntary pitter-patter.

Oh, no. She couldn't let herself go there.

Kai—and romance in general—were off-limits.

She cleared her throat. "Good morning."

"Morning." Gage pushed the box closer. "Help yourself."

The pastries weren't normally on her diet—they had no nutritional value whatsoever—but she grabbed a chocolate-covered one anyway.

Maybe some comfort food would cheer her up.

The first bite nearly melted in her mouth and gave her an instantaneous sugar rush.

Kai stood and poured some coffee for her—black just as she liked it. He set it on the table in front of her, and she thanked him.

"Any updates?" She put her donut on a napkin

and wiped her hands, not wanting to look too eager to demolish the pastry.

Both Kai and Gage already looked wide awake, which indicated to her they'd been up for a while. Last night they'd traded shifts, so they'd each gotten a bit of sleep while the other stood guard.

"No updates on our end." Kai took a sip of his coffee. "Are you still good with going to visit Dr. Jean-Pierre today?"

Tori nodded, the bites of her donut suddenly turning into a brick in her stomach. She wanted to talk to Landon. Wanted to find out answers.

Yet another part of her feared those answers.

Those answers could change the course of her life.

She was hesitant to pull her friend into this. But he'd said Nathan's tests were clear. Had he missed something? That had to be it, right?

"We just going to show up at his office?" she clarified.

"Why don't you call him first?" Kai suggested. "See if we can swing by before he starts work."

"Sure."

"Use my phone. It's encrypted."

She punched in Landon's number, but the phone rang and rang until the voicemail picked up.

She didn't leave a message—just in case.

She lowered the device and turned back to Kai

and Gage. "So I guess this leaves us with a walk-in office visit?"

"I guess that's the best place to start," Kai said. "Let's finish our breakfast, and then we'll hit the road. Sound good?"

She ate the last bite of her donut and chased it down with her coffee. Then she nodded. "We might as well get this over with."

———

Questions circled in Kai's brain as they made the hour-and-a-half drive from their rental house to the west side of Atlanta. They'd brought everything with them, just in case.

Always be prepared. It wasn't just a motto for boy scouts.

All night, Kai found himself constantly rubbing his chest. Was there a device inside him? Something that had the ability to kill him?

Unfortunately, it wasn't the first time he'd asked himself questions like that.

On more than one occasion Larchmont had located him, even though Kai hadn't told his boss where he was going. That had led Kai to wonder how Larchmont was tracking him.

Was it his phone? His vehicle?

Or was it something else? Maybe some kind of

chip inside him?

Kai frowned at the thought.

If that was the case, then Larchmont could find Kai anywhere, anytime. There was no escaping. Freedom would never be an option.

And if Kai did have some type of chip inside him, how would he figure out where it was and how to get rid of it?

He usually didn't live in fear. But the whole idea of this had him shaken.

He sighed and glanced out the window.

As Gage drove, Kai kept his eyes peeled for signs of anyone following them.

He didn't see any suspicious vehicles.

They pulled up to the doctor's office, a building with only one medical practice inside.

Gage put the SUV in Park and turned toward them. "I think you two should go in. I'll wait out here and keep my eyes open for trouble. I don't see how anyone could have followed us, but . . ."

"It's only smart," Kai agreed.

He glanced at his friend, wondering for a moment if Gage ever questioned if he had a chip inside him also. The words sounded too paranoid for Kai to ask aloud. Not right now, at least.

Instead, he climbed from the vehicle and escorted Tori inside.

He'd been thinking about how he would ask Dr.

Jean-Pierre these questions. If he would find this guy trustworthy or not.

As far as he knew, this man had no connection with Project Elevate. The doctor was Tori's friend. He'd even done a background check on the man, but he'd seen nothing suspicious. He was thirty-two. Single. Involved with several charities.

"Did you say you dropped out of medical school?" Kai asked as he walked with Tori toward the building.

He wondered briefly if they had a romantic history as well. But he didn't ask. Figured it wasn't any of his business.

Tori nodded. "That's right. I ran out of money and couldn't get approved for the loans—not without any parents in the picture. I knew it was a longshot when I enrolled, but I thought . . . I don't know. I thought God would provide. And He did. Just in a different way than I envisioned."

"Sounds like you had a good attitude about it, at least." It was impressive, really.

"A bad attitude would only serve to make me miserable. Why do that to myself?"

"Well said."

They approached the receptionist at the front desk of Edgerton Family Practice, and Tori plastered on a smile. She was much more approachable than he was.

"Good morning. I'm not here for an appointment, but I'm an old friend of Dr. Jean-Pierre's. Since I'm in the area, I wondered if he might be able to pop his head out so I could say hi?" Tori shrugged sweetly. "I know it's a little unconventional, but I thought it might be worth a shot."

The receptionist smiled before the edges of her lips dipped down. "Ordinarily, I'd find out for you. But Dr. Jean-Pierre isn't in yet."

"I understand. Do you know what time he's supposed to start work?"

"He was supposed to be here an hour ago."

Tori twisted her neck as if confused. "That doesn't seem like him to be late."

"It's not." The receptionist lowered her voice. "I've tried calling his phone, but he's not answering."

He wasn't answering for his office staff either? Kai mused. That didn't sound good.

Was something going on?

It sounded as if they might need to give the man a visit at his house . . . because Kai didn't like the timing of any of this.

CHAPTER
FIFTEEN

TORI FROWNED. It wasn't like her friend to skip work or to not answer his calls.

She prayed Landon was okay. But a bad feeling lingered inside her.

She told the receptionist thank you. Then she and Kai slipped back out to the car where Gage waited. They climbed inside and gave him the update.

Gage's gaze darkened before he asked, "You have his address?"

"I'm finding it now." Kai typed a few more things into his phone before nodding. "Got it. Let's go. I'll call out directions as you drive."

They left the doctor's office, making several turns until they reached an upscale suburb with two-story houses surrounded by immaculate lawns. A few moments later, they found Landon's house—a well-kept, gray-brick transitional style home.

Kai stared at it before looking back at Tori. "I should go alone. Just in case."

Just in case? She didn't like the sound of that.

Resolve hardened in her, and she grabbed the door handle. "That won't be necessary. I'm going with you."

Landon was her friend. Tori needed to be the one to talk to him.

Kai opened his mouth, as if about to argue, but then he shut it. A second later, he said, "Let me take the lead, at least."

"Fine by me."

They climbed from the SUV and approached Landon's place.

Tori could picture her friend living here. She was so proud of all the good work he'd done.

He'd come from humble beginnings and had to fight each step of the way to get his education. Not only that, but he hadn't gone into medicine for the money or prestige. He'd gone into it because he truly wanted to help others. That had been proven true in the years she'd known him.

He'd constantly put the needs of others above his own, going as far as to volunteer at local low-income clinics while in school, even when he should have been studying.

They climbed the steps to the small portico and knocked on his front door.

There was no answer.

Tori had seen Landon's car in the garage. She'd peered inside the small windows on the top of the doors when she walked by.

Not answering his phone? Not showing up for work? Not answering his door?

"Something's wrong," she murmured. "I'm certain of it."

"Let's check around the outside of the house," Kai said.

Together, they walked around the perimeter, looking for signs of anything that didn't seem right. Reaching the back, they climbed the steps to the expansive deck and peered in the bay windows of his kitchen area.

Tori gasped.

Landon lay on the floor. Based on the blood pooled around his head, he was already dead.

———

As Kai stared at the body on the floor, he sensed Tori's distress.

The man had to be Dr. Landon Jean-Pierre.

Kai had looked the man up earlier. This guy fit the description.

Kai only had a split second to decide what to do.

He could leave and anonymously call 911, assuming the man was dead. That was the easiest solution. That way he didn't have to talk to the police. Didn't have as many opportunities for these guys who were chasing them to find them again.

Or Kai could break inside and make sure that the man was dead while also calling 911. But then he and Tori would need to stick around.

Security cameras were perched on the outside of the house. Even if he decided to take off, the police would see he and Tori's images anyway and come looking for them.

"Kai . . ." Tori looked at him, tears in her gaze.

Decision made.

He grabbed an iron chair from the deck and used it to smash the window in the back door. Carefully, he reached in and unlocked it.

Then he stepped inside, his shoes crunching on the glass against the tile floor.

"Careful," he muttered to Tori.

As if she hadn't heard him, she rushed toward her friend, who lay beside the kitchen table. She knelt next to him and put her finger to his neck.

Kai knew he was gone, though. Blood pooled around his head, and a hole pierced his forehead.

Almost as if a trained professional killer had pulled the trigger.

He didn't say that aloud, however.

Kai pulled out his phone and called 911. As he did, his gaze skimmed the rest of the room, and he spotted the blood spatter on the opposite wall. A better picture of exactly what happened here formed in his mind.

He could imagine the doctor being taken by surprise. Probably before he could even plead for his life, the killer had pulled the trigger—and pulled it with precision.

The doctor would have died instantly.

Then the killer had left as quickly and quietly as he'd come, not leaving a single clue behind.

Kai wished he could spare Tori the sight of the grim scene, but he couldn't. He had to wonder, however, about their past relationship. Had the two of them just been friends? Or had there been more between them?

He supposed it didn't matter. So why was he so curious?

Before he finished the call, Tori looked up at him with grim eyes. "He didn't make it."

Kai slid his phone back into his pocket and stood on the other side of Landon's body. "I'm sorry, Tori."

He had the strange desire to hug her—and he wasn't even a hugger. But he could feel her grief and wanted more than anything to comfort her.

He reminded himself, however, to keep his boundaries in place.

"It's not a coincidence he's dead." Tori's voice cracked. "That he was shot. This wasn't some random break-in."

Kai didn't argue with her.

Most likely, her friend had been murdered because of his association with her and Nathan.

The truth was hard to swallow, but there was no need to deny it.

Somebody—most likely the person behind Nathan's murder—was getting nervous he might be discovered. Dr. Jean-Pierre could have seen something when he examined Nathan that could be used as evidence.

But why wouldn't Tori's friend have told her that? Why keep it a secret?

Unless . . . someone had leveraged something against the doctor to keep his silence.

This person could have panicked and killed Landon in order to protect that secret.

A single tear trickled down Tori's cheek, and past her jaw. "He didn't deserve this."

Again, Kai wanted to reach for her, to offer her some kind of comfort. But he didn't. It took everything inside him to keep his distance.

"You're right," Kai murmured. "Your friend didn't deserve this."

Tori quickly wiped her cheek and drew in a shaky breath as if trying to pull herself together.

She swallowed hard before asking, "Did you see any signs that someone broke in?"

"No, I didn't. There are security cameras. Maybe they picked up on something." However, if someone highly trained did this—as Kai suspected—then there would be no evidence. He guessed that was what police would find.

Just then, sirens began wailing in the distance.

Kai needed to tell Gage what was going on. Then he needed to prepare himself to answer the inevitable questions from first responders. He and Tori needed to get their story straight.

THE POLICE HAD ALREADY QUESTIONED Tori and gotten her contact information. She'd done her best to remain calm and not raise any suspicions as she'd spoken with them.

When they asked her why she'd come by Dr. Jean-Pierre's, she explained that the two of them were former classmates. She told them that she was in town, so she'd swung by for a visit. Kai was simply a friend who'd come along with her.

Just the spiel they'd discussed.

Tori told them she'd seen Landon's car in the garage and had become concerned—especially since he wasn't answering his door or phone. He wasn't the irresponsible type. That was when she got worried and decided to walk around back.

The detective on the scene seemed to believe her story. He didn't eye her suspiciously or ask to take her in for a statement.

Thankfully.

Guilt plagued Tori, and even though she'd tried to push it aside, it was no use.

She couldn't help but feel like this was all her fault.

She knew the truth. Landon had been killed because Tori had gotten him involved in her investigation.

She should have been more careful. However, she'd had no idea it would turn into this. If only she could turn back time . . .

If her theory was true, then Landon had seen something when he examined Nathan. Why hadn't he told her?

Nothing made sense.

Just then, a thin blonde woman Tori had never seen before flew through the front door.

As soon as the woman saw the first responders gathered around someone on the floor, a guttural cry escaped. "Landon!"

The woman darted toward him, but one of the officers caught her and held her back.

She burst into sobs as she peered at Landon.

Tori's throat swelled with emotion at the sight.

Was this Landon's girlfriend? He'd mentioned

last time he and Tori spoke that he'd started to see someone. This must be her.

What was her name again? Tori tried to remember. Natalie?

Maybe.

She and Kai exchanged a glance as they watched the scene unfold.

They would need to talk to her. Though it seemed insensitive, Natalie was their best bet as far as figuring out who might have done this to Landon.

But they couldn't talk to her here in front of everyone.

Besides, Natalie probably had no idea who Tori was. The two had never met, and Tori doubted Landon had mentioned her. They were friends, but not so close that they talked all the time. Tori had helped tutor Landon once, and they'd been like siblings after that.

When the detective on the scene asked Natalie to wait in the living room, Tori saw her opportunity to chat.

Quietly, she lowered herself into the overstuffed chair beside Natalie. She mirrored the woman's body language as she leaned forward with her arms on her knees.

"I'm Tori." She kept her voice soft. "You must be Natalie."

The woman's eyes flashed with recognition. "Landon mentioned you before."

"He did?" Tori probably should have tried to keep the surprise from her voice. But it was too late now.

"He said you were his cheerleader throughout medical school."

Those words caused a small smile to flutter across Tori's lips. "He was a great guy, and I knew he'd be a great doctor. I was right."

Tears filled Natalie's eyes as she nodded. "He loved his job. You're the one who found him?"

Natalie's gaze locked onto Tori's, desperation for answers lingering there.

Tori nodded and told Natalie the same story she'd told the police.

"I just can't believe this." Natalie slowly rocked her head back and forth. "I know we've only been dating a few months. But we had such a strong connection, and . . ."

"Landon said the same about you. I'm so sorry." She squeezed Natalie's hand. "I can't imagine how this would have happened."

"Me either. Who would do this to Landon?"

Tori thought she might have the answer, but she didn't dare speak it aloud. Not without proof, at least.

Instead, she asked, "Did he have any disagreements with anyone lately?"

Tori felt insensitive asking the question, but she had to know.

"No, he was a good guy. You know that. Everyone loved him."

Natalie's words were true. Landon was a likeable guy with a good heart.

But even good guys sometimes had run-ins with the wrong people.

Natalie stared at her, her gaze processing everything. "I assumed this was a random break-in gone wrong or something. You're telling me it wasn't?"

Tori needed to backtrack. "I'm not telling you anything. I'm just deeply concerned over what might have happened. My friend," she nodded at Kai, "does some PI work. He thinks the scene is suspicious."

"PI work?"

She nodded. Tori and Kai had discussed this already. "That's right. I . . . well, I want answers about who did this. I know it seems fast to jump into something like this, but . . ."

"No, I understand. I want answers also." Natalie's eyes suddenly widened. "Now that you mention it . . ."

"What is it?" Tori could hardly breathe as she waited to hear what Natalie was thinking.

"As you know, Landon loves golf. A couple of weeks ago he met this guy at the country club. I think his name was Alfie. The two of them seemed to hit it off. But something about their conversations rubbed me the wrong way."

"How so?"

Natalie frowned. "I don't know . . . they got so close so fast. Alfie said he was a pharmaceutical salesman, and he asked Landon lots of questions that seemed too personal to me."

"Like what?"

She blew out a breath. "I don't know. Like about the hours he worked, what kind of pay doctors in the area made, what kind of patients he saw. Alfie claimed he might want to go back to medical school one day. Maybe that was true . . . but I don't know."

"Anything else?" Tori asked. Right now, there was nothing directly suspicious about the man. She needed to dig deeper.

"There was this one time when Landon and I were out on a date, and Alfie showed up." Natalie frowned as if the memory bothered her. "He claimed it was a coincidence, but I had to wonder . . . he just came on strong, you know?"

"I can imagine."

"And once Landon said something a little strange." Natalie pressed her lips together as if she didn't want to continue.

"What was it?"

"Probably not a big deal, but he said Alfie was super competitive. Like he tried really hard to beat him every game. He liked to get there early. Even prided himself in getting better parking spaces. It was weird if you ask me. But I guess those facts don't tie in with any of this." She let out a soft chuckle. "I'm grasping at straws."

"Maybe," Tori said. "But maybe not."

Was there more to this Alfie guy than what he'd let on?

Tori's gaze met Kai's as he stood across the room, practically making himself disappear in the midst of all the first responders lingering around.

Like a ghost.

Just as he'd been trained.

Despite that, something unspoken passed between the two of them.

They both knew it was absolutely essential that they find answers about Landon's death.

———

Kai waited until he and Tori were dismissed by the police and inside the SUV with Gage before he discussed the situation.

Tori recounted her conversation with Natalie,

ending with, "And I got her phone number, so if we have any more questions we can call her."

"Good work back there," Kai said. "You were great."

He meant the words. Tori had been a total natural talking to Natalie. No part of their conversation had seemed forced or as if she was doing it for her own benefit.

Tori seemed like the type who genuinely cared about people, which was probably what made her such a good nurse.

"So what do we do now?" Gage draped his arm over the seat to address both of them.

"I want to go find this Alfie guy," Kai said. "Maybe he knows something. Or maybe he's a suspect. Either way, he's a place to start."

"We won't know unless we talk to him," Gage said.

Kai glanced at Tori. "Did Natalie give you the name of the country club?"

"She did, but I think finding him is going to be easier said than done," Tori said. "All we know is that he and Landon met at the golf course. Alfie could have been there for the sole purpose of crossing paths with Landon. And if Landon is no longer around, then this guy will have no reason to go back there."

"You could be right, but someone at the country

club might be able to describe him." Kai shrugged. "They might even be able to tell us how to find him. It seems worth a shot."

"I agree," Gage said. "If we can track this guy down, maybe we can find some answers."

"Then what are we waiting for?" Tori glanced at them, a new determination in her gaze. "Let's go."

TORI PUSHED down a shudder of nerves as she stepped into the country club with Kai. Just as before, Gage would remain in the SUV as lookout.

Investigating wasn't normally her type of thing. She liked to help people.

Yet in another way, she supposed she *was* helping someone right now. Just not in the way she normally did.

If something had happened to Landon because of her, she wanted to know.

Kai had already said he'd take the lead, and she was more than happy to let him do that. In fact, he looked as if he were in his element as he transformed into the kind of guy who graced country clubs.

Apparently, putting on facades had been part of their training with Project Elevate.

They strode toward the reception desk. A man with light-brown hair stood there, looking fresh out of college in his white polo shirt and with his easy smile.

"How can I help you? You here to play a round? Maybe enjoy the tennis courts or swimming pool?"

Kai leaned against the counter. "Actually, we have a question, and we're hoping you can help us."

Tori's mind raced as she wondered how Kai would approach this. Would he stick with the truth? Or would he come up with a cover story?

She couldn't think on her feet this quickly to concoct a story.

"What can I do for you?" the man asked.

"A friend of ours plays golf here, and he met up with a man named Alfie," Kai started. "We're trying to figure out who this guy is so we can invite him to our friend's surprise party. Unfortunately, we don't have a last name. But since his first name, Alfie, is pretty unique, we're hoping that you might remember him."

The man let out a "hmm" before shrugging. "I've only been working here a couple of weeks so I'm not going to be a big help."

"Oh, man." Kai clucked his tongue and shook his head. "That's too bad. Is there anyone else who might be able to help?"

The guy thought about it before his eyes lit, and

he snapped his fingers. "You should talk to Daniel. By the time people leave the golf course, everyone thinks of him as their best friend. He has one of those personalities."

"Where can we find this Daniel guy?" Kai asked.

"He's a beverage cart attendant, so you'll see him on the greens."

"Any chance we could go look for him?" Kai lowered his voice and shrugged as if the request was innocuous. "We're not members, but we won't cause a scene."

The man hesitated.

Kai slid a couple of twenties across the desk.

The man glanced around before taking the cash and pocketing it. "Sure, go right ahead. Just don't be too long. I really don't want to lose this job."

"Thank you."

Tori and Kai headed toward the back of the building. When she stepped outside, she took in the scenery a moment. The rolling green hills, the sand traps, the skillfully designed ponds.

She'd never played golf so being in a place like this was totally unfamiliar to her. Kai, on the other hand, looked comfortable as they strode past a line of golf carts and several players about to set out.

"So how are we going to find this Daniel guy?" she murmured as they paused on the greens.

"Actually, we might be in luck today." He nodded

at something in the distance. "Maybe that's our guy right there."

She followed his gaze and saw a man driving toward them in a golf cart stocked with beverages. Based on his broad smile and the way he waved at everyone as he passed, he could very well be Daniel.

"Let's give it a shot," Kai said.

Tori drew in a slow breath and prayed for the best.

Kai plastered on his best smile as he approached the cart. He pulled out his wallet and grabbed a ten-dollar bill. "I'd love some water. Two, please."

"Absolutely." The man took his money, grabbed the water from the cooler, and handed the bottles to Kai. Then he began to get change.

"Don't worry about it," Kai said. "It's all yours."

Another smile stretched across the man's face. "Thanks, man. Appreciate that."

"Hey, listen," Kai started. "Are you Daniel, by chance?"

His smile faded some. "I am."

"Maybe you can help us. We're looking for a man named Alfie. We want to invite him to a surprise party for our friend, but we're having trouble finding him. Do you know him by chance?"

"Alfie? Yeah, man. I remember him. He used to play down here with that doctor guy."

"Dr. Jean-Pierre," Tori added with a hopeful smile. "That's who the party's for."

Word of the doctor's death shouldn't have spread yet so this story should be believable.

"Well, I couldn't tell you much about him. Don't know his last name." Daniel waved at someone else before turning back to them. "But strangely enough, I *did* see him at my uncle's apartment complex the other day."

"Is that right?" Kai tried to keep his voice casual. "Do you mind if I ask which apartment complex? Maybe we could track him down there. I know it's unlikely, but it's worth a shot."

Daniel's smile faded as a touch of caution filled his gaze. "I generally don't tell people where patrons here at the golf course live." He shrugged. "It's a privacy issue, you know?"

"Makes perfect sense," Kai said. "We don't want to ask you to do something that goes against your conscience. We just want to give this guy an invitation. I suppose we could write it out on some paper, and if you see this guy here at the golf course before Friday, maybe you could give it to him?"

Daniel seemed to consider that option also but frowned. "I'd like to say I could do that, but knowing me I'd probably forget."

Kai took a step back. "I just thought it was worth a try. Didn't mean to bother you."

He took Tori's arm and began to lead her away, hoping his bluff would pay off.

They took one step. Then another. And another . . .

"Hey, wait," Daniel called.

Kai suppressed a smile as he turned back toward the man. "Yes?"

"My uncle lives in the New Bridge apartments on East Street. I saw Alfie going into one of the apartments in the same building as my uncle. Building 4C. Second floor. But that's all I know. If anybody asks, you didn't hear this from me."

"Absolutely." Kai gave him a thumbs up. "We'll save you a piece of birthday cake and have either Dr. Jean-Pierre or Alfie bring it to you sometime."

"I'll hold you to that." He raised his hand in a finger pistol.

Kai thanked the man again, but before he walked away he had one more question. "Could you describe this guy?"

"Average height and build. Maybe he has an Indian background—the country, not Native American. Dark thick hair with a touch of curl. He's the kind of guy who gets attention when he walks into a room—not because he's handsome but because he has a big personality."

Kai thanked Daniel one more time before walking back toward the exit.

"I can't believe he told you all that information," Tori murmured.

"I can't either. Someone up above must be looking out for us."

"Certainly sounds like it," she agreed.

Was she a believer? Kai wondered. This was her second mention of God.

And if so, why did that idea excite him so much?

He wasn't sure. But the more he got to know this woman, the more he liked her.

That could be a very dangerous thing.

THEY WASTED no time going to the apartment building Daniel told them about.

Tori was glad they were continuing to move forward, but she had to wonder what the odds were they would find this guy here.

Especially if he was the one who'd killed Landon.

Then again, that theory might be a stretch. Just because Alfie had befriended Landon at the golf course didn't mean Alfie had ultimately killed the doctor. Tori needed to be more open-minded, she supposed.

Still, this guy was their best bet for finding answers right now and, as far as she was concerned, her number one suspect.

Because if the wrong people discovered that Nathan had been seen by Dr. Jean-Pierre, they might have sent someone to get close to her friend in order to find out what he knew.

Then they might have finished him off.

Tori's gut clenched at the thought. She hated the very idea of that happening so much. Hated that Landon had died.

But now she was more determined than ever to find answers.

They pulled up to the apartment complex and found a parking space facing Building 4C. The place was nice and well-kept, with white and black siding, a grassy lawn, and a sprawling lake in the center of all the buildings.

"So what's our plan?" Tori leaned forward between the two front seats. "Do we knock on doors? Do we wait? And if we do see this Alfie guy, what do we even say?"

"First, I'd like to see if this guy is here," Kai said, his voice confident. "To keep an eye on him for a while before questioning him. So right now, we're playing it by ear."

She glanced behind her, tension creeping up her spine. "You haven't seen anyone following us today?"

"I've been keeping my eyes open," Gage said. "No one yet. But if someone did kill the doctor, there's a good chance they were watching his house, waiting for when his body was discovered. We definitely need to be on guard."

That made perfect sense to her. She shivered at the thought.

"Larchmont called." Gage leaned back in his seat, his jaw twitching with unspoken words.

"When?" Tension rang through Kai's voice.

"While you guys were checking out the golf course."

"What did he say?" Kai's words were markedly more clipped. "Did he sound suspicious?"

"I wouldn't say he sounded suspicious," Gage said. "You know he always likes to check on us. But he also always seems to know everything that's going on. It wouldn't surprise me if he knew the two of us are together with Tori down here in Georgia. It wouldn't even surprise me if he knows what we're doing."

"Do you think he planted bugs somewhere? Or trackers?" Tori asked. "Is that how he knows?"

"It's hard to say." Kai shrugged. "I don't know."

Tori's throat tightened. "But if Larchmont is one of the bad guys, and he knows where you are and what you're doing, then . . ."

"Then it could mean trouble," Kai finished. "But I'm not a hundred percent convinced yet that Larchmont is one of the bad guys. Still, I want to be very cautious whenever we speak with him."

Her thoughts continued to race. "You guys trusted this Larchmont guy, right? Do you really think he could betray you like this?"

Kai and Gage exchanged a look, and she knew the answer.

Betrayal was a definite possibility.

And betrayal was a terrible thing to experience. The closer you were to the person who stabbed you in the back, the worse it felt.

She knew that firsthand.

"Larchmont is a very complicated guy," Kai finally explained. "Powerful, wealthy. A bit of a mystery. For the longest time, he's been almost like a father figure to all of us. But he definitely has secrets."

"The question is, what kind of secrets?" Gage added.

Tori didn't like the sound of any of this.

It sounded almost like a game—an entirely dangerous one.

One she never signed up to participate in.

———

The threesome had been sitting in the parking lot for just over an hour. They'd tried to research Alfie by plugging in his address and name, but nothing had popped up.

Finally, their patience paid off.

A man who fit Alfie's description parked in one of the spaces, clicked the key fob to lock his silver Toyota Highlander, and then started toward Building 4C.

Kai sat up straighter as he watched.

"What do we do?" Tori followed the man with her gaze. Then she raised her phone and snapped a picture of him. "Just for good measure."

Kai had already thought everything through. "I'm going to go to the door and see if he'll talk to me. Meanwhile, Gage will go to the back of the building in case the man decides to run. We need you to stay in the car."

"But—" she started to interject.

"We don't know what kind of guy we are dealing with." Kai's voice turned stern. He needed to drive home how important this was. "He could be danger-ous. A killer. The last thing we want to do is to put you in the line of fire."

"But—"

"Gage and I are trained operatives," Kai contin-ued. "We know how to handle situations like this. Do you?"

Tori opened her mouth as if to argue, then shut it again. Instead, she nodded. "It makes sense. I'll stay here."

"Perfect. Lock the doors. If anyone approaches you, lie on the horn and we'll be here. Understand?"

"Understood," she muttered.

She sounded compliant, and Kai prayed she'd truly do what she'd promised. She seemed like someone who was trustworthy and honest.

Once Alfie disappeared inside his apartment, Kai and Gage climbed out. Just as they'd discussed, Gage started toward the back of the building. Even though Alfie's apartment was on the second floor, each unit had a balcony—and someone skilled enough could scale it and run.

Kai had seen it happen before.

He calmly walked up the stairs and paused in front of the door Alfie had entered. He lifted a quick prayer before ringing the doorbell.

He waited but heard nothing on the other side.

He continued to wait.

After several minutes, he bypassed the doorbell and rammed his fist against the door instead. "Alfie, I know you're in there. We need to talk."

Still nothing. Not even any signs of movement inside.

If this guy thought he could hide out and pretend not to be home then he was in for a surprise.

Kai would give the man one more chance before breaking the door down.

He rang the doorbell *and* pounded on the door this time. "Open the door. I'm not going away."

This time, movement sounded inside.

A footfall.

But still, no one answered the door.

Just as Kai braced himself to burst inside, a yell sounded out back.

That was Gage, wasn't it?

They had a runner.

Kai rushed down the steps to help his friend.

They couldn't let this guy get away . . . especially not if he had the answers they needed.

CHAPTER
NINETEEN

TORI STARED at the apartment building, wondering what was happening.

She closed her eyes and prayed Kai and Gage were okay. Every move they made seemed so risky. Had the potential for danger and harm.

She hated everything about this situation.

She couldn't let herself get so focused on this Alfie guy that she let her guard down. If Larchmont —or whoever was behind these acts—was watching them, then he might see this as an opportunity.

She couldn't let that happen.

How had her life gone from a simple one, doing a job she loved, to this?

Not that her life had been perfect before.

There had been Michael, her fiancé. He was a doctor back in Houston, and Tori had caught him cheating on her with another nurse. He'd begged her to try to work things out, but she'd refused—infidelity was a deal-breaker for her.

Three weeks later, her job in Houston had ended, and she'd taken a new assignment in Seattle.

Then there was everything with Nathan.

Knowing someone may have killed both Nathan and Landon caused knots to form in her stomach. How had everything turned into such a nightmare?

She glanced up and saw Kai still at the door. He hadn't gone inside yet.

Exactly what was this Alfie guy doing? What if he emerged with a gun?

How could she step in and help? Her nursing skills might help them after they were harmed, but those skills would do no good in the heat of battle.

Tori glanced behind her, still on edge and unable to let down her guard.

A dark sedan slowly pulled into the parking lot.

She sank lower in her seat and squinted as she tried to make out the car's details.

Was that the same vehicle that had been following them when they were at Nathan's?

She wasn't positive. But the fact the driver drove so slowly through the parking lot raised some red flags.

She glanced back at the apartment building in time to see Kai running down the steps.

Something had happened, she realized.

She looked behind her again, her heart pounding harder.

The sedan slowly came closer to the SUV where she hid.

The dark, tinted windows didn't allow her to see who was inside.

Her gaze swerved back to Kai again.

He darted toward the back of the building.

Alfie must have tried to run. Now Gage and Kai were trying to stop him.

She twisted her neck to look behind her one more time, unsure which direction to focus on.

The sedan was almost directly behind her and going slower than ever.

She looked back at the apartment complex.

Should she blare the horn?

Or was she just being paranoid?

Her choice could mean life or death.

———

Kai darted to the back of the building. As he reached it, he spotted Gage chasing Alfie across the grass near the man-made lake.

The man was surprisingly fast as he darted away.

But so was Gage.

His colleague quickly tackled the man.

Alfie didn't give up. He tried to army crawl out of Gage's grip.

Kai quickly stepped in front of him, stopping the man from going any farther.

Alfie glanced up, and defeat filled his gaze. His shoulders slumped as he went limp on the ground. "Okay, Okay. I'm not going to run anymore."

"That's right. You're not." Kai placed his hands on his hips, not bothering to hide his irritation. "What I'm not sure about is why you ran in the first place. We just wanted to have a conversation."

Alfie scowled, still sprawled on the ground. "Look, I'm going to pay Grant back. I don't know how many times I have to tell you guys."

"Grant?" Kai squinted. "Who is Grant?"

Gage climbed off him and stood, jerking Alfie to his feet.

The man brushed the grass from his jeans and scowled at them again. "Don't play dumb."

"Who is Grant?" Kai repeated, not in the mood for small talk.

Alfie's eyes narrowed even more. "Okay, if you're going to play this game then . . . Grant is a man I owe a lot of money to, thanks to some poor choices I made. He said he'd send his goons after me if I didn't pay in full."

Kai narrowed his eyes. "You're in luck. We're not with Grant."

Uncertainty fluttered through Alfie's gaze. "Then who are you?"

"We're friends of Landon Jean-Pierre," Gage stated.

Alfie's eyes widened before he squinted again. "I know Landon. Nice guy. What about him?"

"He's dead."

"What?" Alfie's mouth dropped open. "When? How?"

Kai wasn't sure if this guy was just a good actor or what. But so far, his reactions seemed pretty believable.

"We found him earlier today," Gage said. "Murdered."

Alfie ran a hand over his face before shaking his head, his entire body tensing. "I can't believe it."

"You're saying you know nothing about it?" Kai clarified.

"Of course, I don't know anything about it!" Alfie's voice rose with frustration. "Why would I?"

"Why don't you tell us a little bit about your friendship with him?" Gage stepped closer. "Because how the two of you met is a little suspicious."

"What's suspicious about it? We both liked golf. There's nothing weird about that."

Gage's expression remained stony. "So you didn't befriend him with ulterior motives?"

"I don't know what kind of world you're living

in, but I'm simply a guy who likes golf." His voice rose with each word. "I was looking for someone to play with, and Landon and I started to talk. We were a good fit. That's the end of the story."

Kai stared at the man another moment, still trying to ascertain whether or not Alfie was telling the truth.

Before he decided, a horn began blasting in the parking lot.

His breath caught.

Tori, he realized.

She was in trouble.

Kai darted toward the sound, praying he wasn't too late.

TORI WATCHED in horror as the sedan stopped behind the SUV where she hid.

The door opened, and a man stepped out.

As soon as she saw him, she sprang into action. She lunged from the back seat across the center console and grabbed the steering wheel. Then she lay on the horn.

She slammed the heel of her hand into the horn several more times, making sure she'd be heard.

What if that man pulled out a gun? If he shot her through the glass?

She almost didn't want to look behind her. But she couldn't stop herself.

The man came into view. Mid-thirties. Stocky. Military-style buzz cut. Square face.

He wore black utility pants and a black shirt.

A gun bulged at his side.

Their gazes met.

The man froze.

He stood beside the SUV just long enough for her to get a better look at his face.

Had she seen him before?

She wasn't sure, but he looked vaguely familiar.

She continued slamming on the horn, desperate to cause a scene.

Suddenly, the man turned on his heel. He darted back to the sedan and hopped inside.

In the blink of an eye, the car squealed away.

Someone darted by, moving so quickly they were like a flash.

Kai, she realized.

He passed her, gun raised as he went after that car.

But he was a few seconds too late.

He paused behind the SUV, watching as the sedan pulled away and muttering something beneath his breath.

Tori knew it was no use trying to catch the driver.

Kai jogged toward her and knocked at the window.

She opened the door.

Only then did she realize how badly she was trembling.

Kai peered at her, concern on his face. "Are you okay?"

She nodded, fully aware that the situation could have turned out so much differently. "I'm fine."

"I'm glad. I was worried. When I heard you honking . . ."

He didn't finish his statement, but Tori could fill in the blanks. His mind had also jumped to worst-case scenarios when he'd thought that something had happened to her.

His concern touched her. They hadn't known each other long, but their experiences over the past forty-eight hours had bonded them.

She swallowed the lump in her throat and reminded herself not to get too attached. That was always a bad idea.

Instead, she asked, "Did you catch the guy? Alfie?"

Kai seemed to snap from whatever heavy thoughts he carried and nodded. "We did. Gage is talking to him now. I'm going to bring him over here so we can talk in private and be close to you, okay?"

Tori nodded, her mind still racing. She wasn't going to argue with that. A part of her still feared the guys in the sedan might come back again.

She slid across the center console to her place in the back seat and rubbed her arms.

This situation wasn't going to get any better, was

it? Not unless they were able to stop these guys. Stop these men who were chasing them. The ones who might have been responsible for her brother's death. For Landon's death.

Kai stepped away but remained close enough to reach her quickly if needed. He motioned to someone just out of sight.

A moment later, Gage appeared, gripping Alfie's arm. He escorted the man to the SUV and shoved him in the front seat. Gage climbed behind the steering wheel, and Kai slid into the back beside her.

Alfie sent her a look of confusion as he glanced back. He clearly had no idea who she was or why she was in the SUV. She didn't have the same "security/tough guy" vibe as Kai and Gage. For all she knew, Alfie might think she was being held captive—kind of like him.

"I don't know why you guys are treating me like a criminal," he muttered. "I'm just a normal guy who was hanging out in my apartment after work."

Silence stretched a moment.

"Now do you want to tell me what's going on?" Alfie's gaze shot back and forth between all of them.

Tori glanced from Kai to Gage, trying to figure out their next move.

Did they believe this guy?

Because she wasn't sure if her instincts said he was trustworthy or not.

"Like we told you earlier, Landon is dead," Kai said. "Murdered. And your name came up during the investigation as a possible suspect."

Alfie's face went pale.

———

Kai was usually pretty good at reading people. But he was having a hard time with Alfie.

The guy seemed sincere. But there was just something about him . . . Kai didn't know if he could trust the man.

"Look, I didn't kill anyone, okay?" Alfie scowled. "Am I free to go and continue my day?"

"Let's say you're telling the truth," Kai said. "How well did you know Landon?"

"Pretty well. We liked to shoot the breeze while we teed off." Alfie rubbed his neck, his hair disheveled and his once-neat shirt now untucked.

"Then tell me about him," Kai continued.

"I don't know how much there is to say." Alfie let out a quick, nervous chuckle. "He was originally from Albany, New York. He was dating a new girl he just met two or three months ago. Said he really liked her. What else do you want to know? I think he told me the name of his favorite pizza place if that would help."

Kai glanced at Tori who nodded, confirming that everything he'd said was true.

Had they gotten this wrong? Had their measures been too aggressive?

Kai wasn't ready to concede.

"Did he ever say anything about any enemies?" Gage asked.

"What?" Alfie's eyes widened. "Who are you guys? Cops?"

"Private security agents," Kai said. "We're looking into what happened to Landon."

Alfie shook his head before running a hand over his face. "I didn't expect that question. But now that you mention it, Landon *did* say he had a patient upset with him."

"Tell us more," Kai said.

"This guy's wife came to see him with a migraine," Alfie said. "Landon prescribed her some meds. But she had a terrible reaction to the pills, which then led to an aneurism. She died. The husband blamed Landon and filed a wrongful death suit against him and the drug manufacturer."

"That's rough," Gage said.

"Landon seemed kind of freaked out," Alfie said. "He talked to me about it since I'm in the pharm world. But this guy—the husband—was over the top. Landon even caught the guy following him a few times and considered hiring personal security or filing a police report about it."

"Why didn't his girlfriend tell us about this?" Tori asked.

Good question, Kai mused.

"He didn't want to freak her out. So he decided to keep it quiet and see if it would blow over. He mentioned something about that once when we were playing golf."

"Then why'd he tell you about it?" Gage asked.

"I don't know, man. Maybe he just wanted to talk about it with someone." Frustration rose in his voice.

The theory seemed viable.

Kai had never considered that the killer could be a patient.

The theory gave him something else to think about . . . but if that was true, then Landon's death would only slow down their investigation—something they couldn't afford.

———

They let Alfie go—after getting his full name and number. But Tori noticed Kai didn't quite apologize for chasing him down. He did, however, seem to soften toward the man the longer they talked.

She wasn't sure if that meant Kai thought Alfie was innocent or not.

She gave him time to sort his thoughts as they drove to a barbecue restaurant.

They hadn't eaten anything since breakfast, and they were all hungry. It had been a long day, and it wasn't going to get any shorter. They still had things they needed to do.

The three of them sat at a corner booth and ordered sandwiches, fries, coleslaw, and drinks.

It wasn't until they got their food that they talked about anything of substance.

"So what do you think?" Tori started before raising her straw to her mouth and taking a long sip of iced tea.

"That's a hard one." Kai lifted his sandwich. "I want Alfie to be our guy. We need to do some more research into him now that we know his last name."

"I have to admit that if he's a liar, he's a good one." Gage shrugged and grabbed a handful of fries.

"I agree," Tori said. "He seemed truly shocked by everything."

"He did." Kai nodded.

Tori shifted in the booth. "But what about this patient he mentioned? The one who's suing Landon? Should we look into him?"

"If one of the doctor's patients did this to him, then this has nothing to do with Nathan or our investigation," Kai said. "It would just be a terrible coincidence."

Why did she find that so hard to believe? Even though she knew they had other pressing matters, the thought of dropping this caused a swell of disappointment inside her.

"Landon's death still seems like maybe something we should look into," Tori said. "It just seems weird to not pursue it anymore. Don't you think?"

Compassion flickered in Kai's gaze before quickly disappearing. "If we run out of other leads, then we can see what we can find out. But I don't think it should be at the top of our priority list now. Let the police see what they can figure out first."

Tori picked up a fry and tapped it against the side of her plate in thought. "I really wanted Landon to examine you both. To *really* examine you and take X-rays."

"He may have been compromised," Kai said softly.

Her throat tightened. "He wasn't that type."

"Then why didn't anything show up during Nathan's examination?" Gage asked.

She dropped the fry. "I have no idea."

She couldn't deny something was amiss. But Landon was one of the good guys . . .

She swallowed hard. She'd think more about that later.

Clearing her throat, she turned back to Kai and Gage. "I think it's important to find out as much information as we can about what's going on inside your bodies."

"Now that you mention it . . ." Kai pulled some keys from his pocket and dangled them in the air. "I snagged these at Landon's house."

Her eyes widened. "Are those . . . ?"

"Keys to the doctor's office, as well as his security badge."

Tori's eyes widened. "You want to break into the office?"

"Break-in sounds harsh." Kai shrugged nonchalantly. "I just want to use the equipment. You know how to, right?"

"How to use the X-ray machine? I mean, yes . . . but—"

"Then tonight? After hours?" Kai stared at her as he waited for her answer.

She blew out a long breath. She wasn't sure what she thought about this idea. But did they have any other viable choices right now?

Not really.

She licked her lips, apprehension brewing inside her. "I suppose we could do that. But if we're caught . . ."

"We won't be caught."

Tori stared at him a moment, hoping another idea would hit. None did.

Still, she could lose her nursing license if they

were caught.

But Kai insisted they wouldn't be. Still, how could he know that for sure?

He couldn't.

Was the risk worth it?

It would mean possibly saving Kai's and Gage's lives. Their well-being was more important than her career.

She swallowed hard and nodded. "Then, okay. I guess we have our solution. We'll go and take some X-rays. What do we do until then?"

Kai let out his own breath. "Thank you. I know you have a lot at stake."

"I just have to focus on what's more important right now."

He nodded and glanced at his food, his appetite seeming to wane. "I got the license plate of that car that pulled up behind you at the apartment complex. I would like to run it."

Gage pulled out his laptop from the backpack he'd brought with him. "I can do a quick search."

"How?" Tori asked.

"Thanks to our job, we have access to tools that the average everyday person doesn't—including running license plates," Kai explained.

Kai called the plate out to Gage, and Gage typed it in.

"This will take a moment," Gage murmured.

"Could you look up Blackstone on this program also?" she asked. "I did an internet search, but I couldn't find anything."

"I already tried," Kai told her. "There's no footprint showing that the company even exists."

Her lip twitched in a frown. "Go figure."

While the program did its thing, they continued to eat.

Tori had to admit that the food was good. Really good. She'd been hungrier than she'd thought. The iced tea, as it flowed over her tongue, brought her a surprising delight—something she welcomed amid everything else that had happened.

She'd take whatever small pleasures came her way. They were like gifts in the midst of walking through fire.

"I've got something." Gage's eyes lit, and he straightened.

Tori set her tea down and turned toward Gage, holding her breath as she waited to hear what he had to say.

"WHO IS THE VEHICLE REGISTERED TO?" Kai's spine stiffened as he waited to hear what Gage had found out.

His colleague stared at his computer. "A man named Howard Monarch."

Kai leaned back, almost disappointed at the news. "I've never heard of him."

"I'll see what else I can find out." Gage typed several more things into his laptop.

Kai tried to be patient as he waited to hear more about the man who owned that vehicle.

Because if Kai hadn't gotten to Tori when he did . . . he hated to think about what might have happened. His muscles hardened at the thought.

Just as Kai finished his meal, Gage's computer dinged the results. "Looks like Howard owns a tech firm here in Atlanta called Broadreach. But other than that, there's not a lot popping up about him—nothing controversial, at least. I'm going to have to dig a little deeper."

"What about Alfie?" Tori asked. "Could you do a search on him as well, especially now that you know his last name and address?"

"Of course." Gage typed something else in. "He's from Pensacola. Dad was military. Parents divorced. His mom is a Botox expert. He works in the pharmaceutical industry. Never been married. It looks like his story checks out."

All of that sounded normal. So why was Kai still bothered?

Maybe because Alfie's explanation seemed too simple. Maybe that was because he'd operated in a complex world of covert missions and espionage—a world where nothing was ever that simple.

He glanced out the window at the darkening sky. If they were going to enact the next part of their plan, they needed to do it soon.

"You still want to break into the office?" Tori asked, almost as if reading his thoughts.

"I need to know the truth," he told her. "You think they're closed yet?"

She glanced at her watch, her expression pensive. "It's past six. They should be."

Kai's gaze slid from Tori to Gage as he nodded.

"Then let's get a plan together as to what we're going to do when we get there."

————

After they finished eating, Tori, Kai, and Gage had hit the Walmart across the street to buy more appropriate clothing before their outing tonight.

Tori couldn't deny she was nervous—about everything.

But sometimes, risk was necessary. This was one of those times, she reminded herself.

By the time they checked out it was past nine p.m.

Kai and Gage had indicated that anytime past ten would be ideal for breaking into the building. First, they needed to be sure that no one else was working late or lingering nearby.

They climbed back into the SUV and, before they took off, Gage grabbed his phone.

"I have more information on Howard," Gage started. "Broadreach is a cybersecurity company and . . . it turns out they're under contract with the government."

"Do they have something to do with Project Elevate?" Tori asked.

"Hard to say."

"If not, why would someone who owns a cyberse-curity company be following me?" Tori asked. "I pretty much hate technology. I don't have any top-secret files or even a money trail to follow."

"That's an excellent question. I'm not really sure." Gage turned the screen toward her. "You ever seen him before?"

Tori stared at the picture of a sixty-something man with a balding head, a leery look in his eyes, and a tight smile.

"I've never seen him before," she said. "He isn't the guy who approached me while I was in the SUV yesterday."

"I'm sure he has men," Kai said.

"He has men following us?" Tori clarified. "Is that how they found us at Alfie's apartment building?"

"Good question." Kai pressed his mouth closed, his jaw muscles visibly tightening.

"Let's go stake out the doctor's office." Gage started the engine. "See if everyone's gone. Then let's get this over with."

Dread pooled in Tori's gut at the thought of it. She didn't want to do this. Didn't want to be caught breaking in.

But she knew it was the only way.

However, another bigger thought loomed over her.

If these men who were following them had located them once, they could do it again.

How would things end next time?

CHAPTER
TWENTY-TWO

THEY WAITED outside the doctor's office thirty minutes to make sure no one was inside.

Though all the lights were off, one car remained in the parking lot.

Kai wondered if someone at the office had gotten a ride home and would pick up the remaining vehicle in the morning. It made the most sense.

Ideally, no one should be here. The last thing they needed was for someone to return in the middle of their covert mission.

Gage had already used a program on his laptop to turn off the security system and cameras so they wouldn't be caught that way. They'd found the blueprints of the place as well, so they could figure out where to go.

As they sat in the SUV, Kai glanced at Tori, and a rush of concern rippled through him.

He knew she didn't want to do this, that she was uncomfortable at the thought of breaking into a doctor's office. He could appreciate that. If there was any way they could do this without her, he would tell her to stay put.

In reality, Kai could probably figure out how to use the X-ray machine. But he wanted to be certain the procedure was done correctly. That meant he needed Tori.

He touched her arm as she sat beside him.

She flinched, clearly lost in another world.

"Sorry," she murmured.

"It's okay," Kai told her. "You sure you're ready for this?"

She nodded even though she looked shaky. "Ready as I'll ever be."

"We'll keep you safe," Kai assured her.

That got a faint but quick smile out of her. "I know."

"Let's go guys," Gage said before opening his door.

They scanned the parking lot one more time to make sure no one was watching.

It was clear.

On the count of three, they ran toward the side door of the building.

While Kai worked on the lock, Gage placed a camera near the door so they could monitor the outside of the building.

A moment later, a click sounded, and the door released.

They were in.

Now came the hard part—discovering the truth.

———

Tori's thoughts swirled as she walked into the eerily quiet doctor's office.

It wasn't as if she'd never been in a doctor's office this late, after hours. But it had always been for professional reasons.

Not because she'd broken in.

Every time she started to have cold feet, she remembered Nathan.

She could do this for him.

She, Kai, and Gage wound down the hallway. Past the check-in desk. Into the clinical area.

So far so good.

When Gage said that he'd disabled all the security cameras, she prayed he was correct.

Because it would be hard for her to find out answers about Nathan if she was in prison.

Tori pointed down another hallway. "Right here.

This is the radiographic imaging room, where the X-ray machine should be located."

Gage remained on guard outside the door while Kai and Tori stepped inside.

Only then did they turn on the lights. Tori blinked against the brightness as her eyes adjusted.

In front of her stood the X-ray machine.

That piece of equipment could give her the answers she so desperately wanted.

Equipment that should have shown Landon that something wasn't right with her brother.

She still couldn't figure out why he would have lied.

Tori glanced at Kai one more time. "Are you sure you want to do this?"

Because really, the results would affect him more than they would affect her.

Depending on what she found out about him, the course of his life could change. It was a big deal and not something to be taken lightly.

"I'm sure," Kai reassured her.

Drawing in a deep breath, she used Landon's badge to turn on the machine and boot up the computer. Then she had Kai take off his belt, empty his pockets, and lie on the table.

Once he was situated, she glanced at him again. On a whim, she reached over and squeezed his hand. A rush of nerves fluttered through her.

"Whatever happens, whatever we discover, it's going to be for the best," she assured him. "It's better to know than not to know, right?"

"Absolutely."

But Tori thought she saw a flash of hesitation in his gaze. Anyone in his shoes might have a moment of questioning if this was the right thing or not.

And Kai, even though he might be a super soldier, was no different.

She lowered the X-ray machine into position.

Then she stepped back to the computer and placed her trembling hand over the keyboard, ready to start.

"Okay, take in a deep breath and hold it," she told Kai.

Then she began capturing images of his bones . . . and anything else that might be hidden beneath his skin.

KAI'S LUNGS felt surprisingly tight as he waited for Tori to move the X-ray machine from overtop him.

Her presence, however, brought him a sense of calm.

It was a strange thing since he'd been through so much—battles, near-death experiences, and even more horrific things he wished he could forget. But being in a doctor's office always gave him a sense of panic.

Kai figured it went back to those experiments done on him.

Most of them he'd blocked from his thoughts. But his subconscious still knew. His body remembered.

Tori took his hand and helped him sit up. She left

a hand on his shoulder as she peered at him, a nurturing look on her face. "You feel okay?"

Kai nodded. "I'm fine."

"Good." She dropped her hand.

As soon as it was gone, he instantly wanted it back.

Which was a crazy thought.

He wasn't the type who needed a woman in his life or any form of close relationship. He had his job to keep him busy.

But what if his job wasn't enough? It wasn't the first time he'd asked himself that question. But he usually dismissed it.

If he was smart, he would dismiss it now also.

"How long until we can see the images?" He tried to redirect his thoughts.

"We can view them on the computer now."

He walked with her toward the desk.

Tori punched in a few things before the images appeared on the screen and murmured, "Here we are."

Kai stared at the black-and-white X-rays.

He saw all the normal things. His rib cage, breastbone, collarbone, and part of his spine.

But those things weren't what made him pause.

No, it was the small circle near his heart that caught his attention.

It was just as Tori had suspected—a pacemaker or another device of that sort.

His heart raced faster at the thought.

"Kai . . ." Tori said softly. "I'm sorry, but there's more."

He looked to where she pointed to something on his shoulder. Something he hadn't even noticed because he'd been so distracted by the piece of metal near his heart.

He squinted. "What is that?"

She used the computer to enlarge the image. "It's small, almost like a chip."

"You mean . . . like a tracker?" Lead formed in his stomach at the thought.

She nibbled on her bottom lip as if trying to cover up a frown. "Maybe."

His fears were right. Someone *had* been tracking his every move.

At the flip of a switch or the push of a button, someone could also kill him.

Kai had a hard time stomaching that thought.

———

Tori wanted to pull Kai into a hug. Wanted to do something to offer him some comfort.

But she didn't feel like it was her place.

Yet another part of her felt connected to him, like maybe the action wouldn't be weird.

Despite that, she held back and remained professional.

"We should check Gage as well," Kai murmured, still staring at the image. "I can take his place and guard the building."

Tori nodded solemnly. "Okay."

They opened the door, and Kai didn't say anything to Gage. The two gave each other a look as they switched places.

She directed Gage to lie down so she could get started.

"You found something, didn't you?" Gage's voice didn't show any emotion as he lay there and asked the question.

"We did," Tori told him. "But that doesn't mean there's something in you too."

However, they both knew that the chances were if Kai had something then so did Gage.

Several minutes later, the results showed that Gage had the exact same implants as Kai.

"I can't believe this." Gage raked a hand through his hair. "They've been hiding this from us. Certainly, other doctors have seen this, but they haven't said anything."

"It sounds like the people you work for have a lot

of others under their thumb." Tori kept her voice gentle, not wanting to stir up any more emotions.

"You can say that again," Gage said the words through gritted teeth. "Next time I talk to Larchmont . . ."

Tori couldn't blame him for the reaction. She would feel the same way in his shoes.

But seeing this, she knew Nathan must have had the same objects inside him.

Whoever had done the autopsy on him had chosen not to report it.

And so had Landon.

Her hands fisted at the thought.

There was a massive cover-up going on here by the military. It was the only thing that made sense.

A new resolve formed in Tori. Nothing would stop her from finding out the truth and exposing the people involved.

A knock sounded on the door, and Gage opened it.

Kai stood there, his earlier confusion gone and replaced by concern. "I saw a shadow move outside the building on the camera feed."

He held up his phone, where he monitored the exterior of the doctor's office.

Tori's pulse quickened. "You think someone followed us here?"

"Knowing what I know now—yes."

More fear ratcheted through her. "What are we going to do?"

"We need to get out of here." Kai squared his shoulders as he shoved his phone back into his pocket. "And we need to do it very carefully."

CHAPTER
TWENTY-FOUR

"GAGE, MAKE SURE TORI IS SAFE," Kai rushed as his muscles bristled and his adrenaline pumped. "I'm going to try to hold these guys off."

"Can't we just all stick together?" Panic raced through Tori's voice, and she froze, looking like a deer caught in headlights.

Kai locked gazes with her, needing to drive home his point. "These guys are trained, and they're armed. It's better if we split up. If we can all get out of here without being seen, that would be perfect. But in my world, perfect doesn't exist."

He didn't give her time to argue. Instead, he nodded at Gage.

His colleague took Tori's arm and led her in the opposite direction.

As soon as Kai took a step down the hallway, he saw a shadow move in the distance.

Someone was definitely inside. They'd been tracked. Again.

Kai started to duck back around the corner when gunfire rang out.

A bullet lodged into the wall right next to him.

This guy was shooting at him.

Kai dropped low and grabbed his own gun.

Using the wall for cover, he fired back.

"It's pointless for you to try to run," the man yelled. "Might as well give up now."

Kai didn't answer, didn't give away his location. Instead, he remained near the corner, waiting for his opponent's next move.

As soon as Kai heard the guy coming close, he slammed his hand down.

But the man ducked out of the way, almost as if he'd been expecting the move.

The butt of Kai's gun barely skimmed the man's head.

The man grabbed Kai's arm, and Kai's gun fell to the floor.

Wasting no time, Kai swung his leg and hit the other man's gun out of his hand also.

They were on equal fighting terms now.

They faced off with each other, both in a crouched fighting pose.

"You don't want to do this," Kai growled.

"You should have left this alone."

Kai needed to keep his eyes wide open. He didn't know how many friends this guy had brought with him, and he didn't want to be taken by surprise.

But he had a feeling there were just two men who'd followed them inside.

This man who was in front of him now and another man who was probably trying to track down Tori.

Kai prayed Gage was able to get her out of here.

His opponent took the first swing.

Then the hand-to-hand combat began.

———

Tori's heart nearly stopped when she heard the gunfire.

What was going on? What if that bullet had hit Kai?

She started to stop, to turn around.

But Gage held her arm tight. "We can't."

"We can't leave Kai to fight this alone." She pulled against him.

He didn't budge. "We need to make sure you're safe."

Gage started to pull her again when she dug in

her heels. "Then put me somewhere safe. You go back and help him."

Gage stared at her, contemplating her request.

A yell sounded in the distance, followed by a crash.

Tori gasped, her mind going to worst-case scenarios.

Kai . . .

What was happening?

Gage's eyes hardened with resolve.

Decision clearly made, he pushed her into the reception area. "Under the desk. Don't come out unless I tell you. Understand?"

She nodded and did as he told her. Gage pushed the chair in after her and then put his fingers over his lips to motion for her to be quiet.

As he stepped from the room, another footfall sounded.

And it wasn't Gage's.

Grunts followed. The sound of flesh hitting flesh. Bodies hitting walls. People moaning.

Tori pressed her eyes closed and told herself not to move.

She'd promised Gage she wouldn't. As much as she'd like to think she could help, she knew there wasn't much she could do. She'd only get in the way.

All she could do was pray—which was the most important thing. *Dear Lord, be with Gage. Be with Kai.*

Keep them safe. Protect them. Cover them. Make our enemies stumble. Blind them and trip their steps.

As Tori heard another groan, she pulled her knees closer.

If that man managed to take out Gage, he might come for her next.

What would she do then?

She'd have no choice but to fight. She knew her efforts probably wouldn't do much good, but she'd give it everything she had.

The next instant, more gunfire sounded.

Her pulse quickened, feeling like it might pound out of control. She could hardly breathe as she tried to imagine what was happening out there.

But maybe it was better if she didn't imagine. Too many horrid scenarios rushed through her head.

Then it suddenly got quiet.

Someone walked toward her.

The question was—was it Gage or Kai?

Or was it one of the men who'd been sent here to destroy them?

TWENTY-FIVE

CEMENT FILLED TORI'S LUNGS.

If only she'd thought to grab something to defend herself with . . . maybe she could have at least bought herself some time as she fended off the bad guys.

Now she'd be at the mercy of whoever was in the room with her.

She wanted to press her eyes shut. To disappear.

If only that were possible . . .

Footsteps stopped in front of her.

Time seemed to pause.

All she could hear was her heart beating.

Who was standing there, mere feet away?

Gage? Kai? Or someone with sinister motives?

Her lungs froze as she waited.

Please, God . . .

She forced her eyes open.

Gage's face appeared.

The air left her lungs in a whoosh.

It was him. He was okay.

Thank You, Jesus!

But what about Kai?

Gage reached out his arm. "We need to go. Now."

Tori grabbed his hand, and Gage pulled her from under the desk. Together, they dashed from the office and down the hall.

A few seconds later, Kai appeared, running beside them.

She glanced at the floor at one of the men who'd infiltrated the office. He lay unconscious, blood drizzling from his forehead.

She carefully stepped over him. But Gage moved fast. Really fast. She hardly had time to think about anything.

The next instant, they were out the door. Gage grabbed the camera. Then they sprinted across the parking lot.

They jumped into Gage's SUV and squealed away from the building.

Tori's thoughts could hardly catch up with her actions.

Before they could have any real conversation, Gage pulled off the highway down a less-traveled road. Then he turned again and again until finally they were on a country lane. He pulled between some trees, out of sight from anyone passing.

He cut the engine and turned to them. "Everything okay?"

Tori nodded, even though she wasn't sure at all that everything was okay. Her head was still spinning. "Who were those guys?"

"There'll be time to ask questions later." Kai pulled something from his pocket. "First, I need you to remove the trackers from me and Gage."

Her eyes widened when she saw the scalpel in his hands. Panic fluttered through her.

Had she heard him correctly? "What?"

"You heard me. I need it out of me." Kai glanced at Gage. "We need to tell the rest of the guys about this also. We're all being tracked and are at the mercy of whoever is behind this . . . this . . . this experiment."

The impact of his words hit Tori, making her heart stammer even more.

Kai handed her the scalpel he must have grabbed from the doctor's office.

Her hands trembled as she held it.

Could she do this? What if she messed up somehow and made things worse?

As Kai stared at her, Tori realized she didn't have much time to figure out exactly what she wanted to do.

———

As they stood on the side of the country road, surrounded by woods, Kai's thoughts raced.

He had to make Tori realize just how important this was. Now that he knew this chip was there, he couldn't go another moment with it implanted inside him.

He turned to face her more fully. "We'll never get away if we have these chips inside us. They'll be able to find us anywhere. They'll be able to find us right now."

Tori stared at him with wide eyes. "It's not going to feel good."

"I can handle it," he reassured her.

"I . . . I don't have any other medical supplies. We need some antiseptic or something to clean you up. And I'll need to stitch you up afterward—"

"We can worry about that later, after the chips are out."

She hesitated another moment before offering a shaky nod. "Okay."

Relief swept through him. Kai knew she was reasonable, that she'd be able to see the importance of this.

He just wasn't sure how long it would take her to have that realization. Thankfully, it had come sooner rather than later.

"We're going to need to sit in the back of the SUV," she told him. "I'll need some space and a steady hand. And what about tweezers? Do either of you guys have something I could use?"

"I don't have tweezers, but there's an old pair of pliers back there," Gage said. "Would that work?"

"An old pair?" She swallowed hard again. "If that's all we've got, then I guess I can make it work. But they have to be sterilized first."

"I grabbed some alcohol wipes, so I'll clean it up," Gage told her.

They walked around to the back, and Gage opened the hatch. Kai sat on it and pulled his shirt off. The dome light from the vehicle fell softly on his shoulders. Then Gage pulled out his phone and turned on the flashlight.

Tori was still trembling as she turned to Kai.

He understood how this would be unnerving. But they had no other choice.

"You can do this." Kai believed those words. Tori *could* do this. She was more than capable.

"I know, it's just that . . . without anything to numb this—"

"You don't worry about me." Kai turned and locked gazes with her. "All I care about is getting this out. You can understand that, right?"

She sucked in a breath before nodding slowly,

seeming to center herself. Then she ran her fingers over his collarbone and shoulder.

"You feel anything?" he asked quietly.

"I don't." She took an alcohol wipe and sanitized the scalpel. Then grabbed another wipe and ran it against Kai's skin. "The X-ray showed it was in this area. It must be in there pretty deep."

"I'll be okay," he tried to reassure her.

But her breathing was a little too shallow for his comfort.

"Here goes," she murmured.

The scalpel sliced into his skin.

He gritted his teeth and closed his eyes.

Yes, it hurt.

But Kai would bear whatever pain necessary if it meant getting this chip out of him.

TWENTY-SIX

TORI HAD DONE IT.

Twenty minutes later, the chips had been removed from both Kai and Gage.

Using a small first aid kit Tori found in the SUV, she'd cleaned the cuts the best she could and put bandages on them. That would work until Kai and Gage could get stitches—unless they didn't care about scarring. But really, they needed stitches so infection wouldn't set in.

Emotionally, it had been one of the hardest things she'd ever had to do as a nurse. Thank goodness, it was over.

As soon as Kai's chip had been removed, he'd taken it, walked to a rock, and smashed the device with his foot.

Gage had done the same.

Tori could rest assured they wouldn't be tracked now.

She shivered at the nighttime around them. The woods were dark and silent, other than the sound of crickets and an occasional owl hooting or frog croaking. The air had turned cooler and brought with it the scent of decaying leaves and old wood.

At least they were alone. No one had found them. No one seemed to be watching—for the moment.

"Should we go back to the house?" she asked after she cleaned her hands with another wipe.

"That location has been compromised." Kai tugged his shirt back on. "We can't go back there. We'll find a hotel for the night instead. Then we can all talk again."

"And I can stitch you guys up."

"Yes, but for right now, let's get out of here." Kai paused and glanced around before looking back at her. "I think we can all agree that it's been a long day."

Tori couldn't argue that.

If only there was somewhere she could go where she'd feel safe.

———

Thirty minutes later, Kai, Tori, and Gage were in a

two-bedroom suite. The place was pricier than they'd wanted, but the location was good.

Kai hoped with those chips out of their bodies that they wouldn't be found, at least for a while. He'd watched on the drive here, and he hadn't seen anyone following them.

Once inside the room with the door locked, Tori collapsed on a couch, her limbs shaky.

He knew today had been tough on her. It had been tough on all of them. The difference was she hadn't trained for circumstances like these. He and Gage had.

Plus, her friend had died, she'd cut chips out from their bodies, broken into a doctor's office, and been chased by gunmen.

He slowly lowered himself onto the cushion beside her. "Are you okay?"

She raked a hand through her dark hair, leaving it disheveled. "My head is just still spinning from everything."

"That's to be expected." He wished he could put her at ease. But he didn't want to give her false reassurances either.

Gage paused near the door. "I'm going to run to the store. Do we know how we're doing on money?"

Kai had thought about that also. Since they were paying in cash, everything was more complicated. But he hadn't wanted to stress Tori out by bringing up any of those issues. She had enough on her mind as it was.

"If we spend carefully, we'll have enough for a couple more days," Kai said. "We can always withdraw more from our accounts."

Gage cocked his head. "Except doing that will let people know where we are."

"Right now, they already know the general area we're in," Kai reminded him.

"That's true." Gage let out a breath.

Tori nibbled on the side of her lip before frowning. "I'm sorry I put you guys in this position."

"None of this is your fault," Kai reassured her. "I'm glad you came to me with what you knew. Maybe we'll finally get some of the answers we deserve."

She nodded, though she didn't look convinced.

Kai knew things just might get harder before they got easier.

In the meantime, none of them were safe.

TORI STARED at Kai a moment after Gage left. What was he thinking about right now?

She'd seen something in his gaze earlier, almost as if he wanted to say something but stopped himself. What was that about?

Maybe it was about how he would be better off right now if the two of them hadn't met. She knew he said he wanted answers. But did anyone really want their life to be turned upside down like this?

Kai seemed to realize Tori was staring at him, and he tilted his head, a curious look in his gaze.

"What? Do I have something on my face?" His voice sounded surprisingly lighthearted.

"I feel like you and Gage are real-life Jack Reachers or something."

A half smile curled his lips. "Jack Reacher isn't real, and we are. Reality can be stranger—or just as strange—as fiction."

"I can't even imagine what it must be like to live like you do." She pulled her knees to her chest as she continued to observe him.

His gaze drifted to the distance. "Sometimes, I don't think I know who I am. Even more so now that I'm learning more about things that were done to me without my permission."

"It's got to be a lot."

Kai leaned back on the couch, a new heaviness in his gaze.

Tori was glad he wasn't hiding how he felt but being real with her. The easy route to go would be to pretend like he was unbothered.

After a couple of moments of silence passed, she asked, "What are you thinking about?"

His expression remained stony as he said, "Those guys who came after us at the clinic . . . something about them is bothering me."

Tori shifted toward Kai, propping her elbow on the couch and leaning her head against her hand. "What do you mean?"

"I don't know. It's one of those things I can't pinpoint. It's more of a gut feeling."

"What is that gut feeling telling you?"

"I'm going to sound crazy." He paused, his jaw tightening. "But I almost feel like . . . they're like me."

Her breath hitched. "Like you as in former military?"

He shook his head. "No, you said your brother went through the same training I did. Only I never knew about him. In fact, I thought my colleagues and I were the only ones who'd gone through the program. That's what we were told. But what if there was a second generation of recruits that we were never told about? Or what if my colleagues and I were the second generation and others came before us?"

The thought was daunting . . . but not necessarily surprising. "I suppose that could be a possibility. Maybe the people in charge realized things they did wrong, and they decided to start over . . . more than once."

"But why wouldn't they tell us?" Kai swung his head back and forth as if perplexed.

She let out a long breath. "Either they thought it wasn't important for you to know or they were trying to hide something."

"Bingo. There's way more to this."

"What if you talk to your boss? Larchmont, right?" Tori asked. "Do you think he would tell you the truth?"

"Right now, I wouldn't believe anything he might tell me. I don't trust him."

She rubbed her arms, chilled by the words she was about to say. But she couldn't stay quiet. "The other thing is . . . those guys who attacked us . . . they weren't good guys."

"Or maybe they *are* good guys, good guys who were led to believe that *we're* the bad guys."

Tori's head spun with the thought.

But she couldn't deny what Kai was saying.

There was a good chance he was absolutely right.

And that thought was terrifying.

———

It had felt good to talk to Tori.

Throughout Kai's life, he hadn't found many people he could open up to like this. Something about Tori made her easy to talk to.

However, he worried about keeping her safe. More than anything, he wished she wasn't involved in this. That she was tucked out of harm's way.

But safety was an illusion right now. There was no turning back time. They'd started this mission and needed to complete it.

He stared at Tori a moment, words wanting to form on his lips. Words he hadn't considered saying in a long time.

I'm starting to care about you.

You're different from anyone else I've ever met.

Your tenacity and bravery are admirable.

He licked his lips. Maybe he should take the plunge and tell her. Take a chance. Forget about his hesitancies.

Opening up about his feelings wasn't something he'd ever really thought he would do.

"Kai?"

He snapped from his thoughts, and Tori's face came into view. Her beautiful face. Her concerned eyes.

This was the perfect opportunity to talk to her.

"Yes?" he answered.

"What are you thinking about now?"

He shifted in his seat, about to take the plunge. "Tori, I—"

Before he could finish, the door rattled then opened. Gage strode inside, several plastic bags in hand. "I got everything we need."

He set the bags on a nearby table—totally oblivious to the conversation that had almost taken place.

Maybe it was better this way. Keeping this impersonal would be the wisest thing to do. Developing feelings while working protective detail was a bad idea.

If Kai kept his thoughts to himself instead of voicing them aloud, maybe he could ignore them. He knew his logic was flawed, but he clung to it at the moment.

Still, he couldn't deny that he was disappointed.

Kai gave Tori an apologetic look before walking toward his colleague. Gage had gotten clothes and toiletries just as requested. And he'd found the suturing kit Tori had asked him to pick up.

He tossed it to her. "You ready for this?"

She stared at the kit before shrugging. "The question is: Are you ready for this?"

"Let's just get it over with."

"Start with Kai," Gage said. "I'm going to hop in the shower. By the time I get out, maybe it'll be my turn."

Kai stripped his shirt off, feeling unusually self-conscious about it. Not about the way he looked but about being in such close proximity to Tori.

He really was developing feelings for her, wasn't he?

The realization was strange. He wasn't normally the type who was interested in any type of relationship.

But something about Tori was different. She somehow made him feel . . . like a better person. The future somehow seemed more fulfilling when he thought about having her in it.

As she threaded a needle, he sat in front of her, all too aware of her presence behind him. When she touched his shoulder a moment later, his skin turned to fire.

All his doubts were gone.

He was in trouble.

Big, big trouble.

TORI DIDN'T USUALLY GET nervous like this when stitching someone up.

She'd done it enough times to remain professional.

But her throat kept going dry as she stared at Kai's muscular back and biceps.

Why did part of her just want to wrap her arms around him in a big hug?

And not just a friendly hug to comfort him.

But a hug that would show how much she was beginning to care about him.

She couldn't stop thinking about their earlier conversation. About the possibility that those guys who'd come after them were a part of the same program. That maybe they thought that Kai and Gage were the bad guys.

If these soldiers had been put through the same rigorous training Nathan and Kai had told her about, then there could definitely be a lot of programming and brainwashing involved.

What exactly were these men capable of?

She still couldn't get over the audacity of someone putting a GPS chip in their shoulders.

That wasn't to mention the pacemaker-like device near their hearts . . . a device that had the ability to end their lives in a split second.

She couldn't stop thinking about the possibility. Was that truly what had happened to Nathan?

What if it also happened to Kai and Gage?

Tori shuddered and refocused on her task.

She couldn't go there. Not now.

"Hold tight. Here goes." She inserted the needle through Kai's skin.

He barely flinched.

This would take probably three stitches. If there was a way they could eliminate a few potential problems and obstacles, then that was exactly what they needed to do.

Even though Tori knew she was incapable of protecting Kai or Gage, that was all that she wanted to do—to protect them.

The idea seemed ludicrous, that someone like her could protect super-trained soldiers. But she knew she'd do everything in her power to keep her new friends safe.

In the short time since she'd come to know Kai and Gage, their experiences had bonded them.

Now they were all in this fight together.

And Tori wasn't about to give up.

———

Kai's thoughts continued to race as he tried to ignore the sting of the needle Tori used.

He knew they were just skimming the surface of everything involved with Project Elevate. He and his colleagues had only been told things on a need-to-know basis.

But this went much deeper. Somehow, he needed to find answers.

When Tori finished the last stitch and placed the bandage over Kai's wound, he turned to her.

As he did, their gazes caught. Something passed between thcm.

Tori felt the same way he did, didn't she?

The realization sent a thrill through him.

But nearly as quickly as he felt the thrill, the feeling disappeared like a shadow in bright light.

Kai knew he had no future with Tori, not with his past and everything he'd been through.

He wasn't even sure he could trust himself

around her. What if there were things happening inside his body he didn't even know about? That X-ray hadn't scanned his brain. What if there was a chip there too that could make him act a certain way at someone's beck and call?

And what if that meant he could turn against Tori without even realizing it?

Those were all chances he couldn't take.

That wasn't to mention the fact that if someone wanted him dead, they could stop his heart at a moment's notice. That could leave Tori exposed and vulnerable.

No, Tori being with him was too risky.

He pulled away, raising an imaginary—and impenetrable—wall between them. "Thank you."

She straightened, seeming to read his body language. The disappointment in her gaze was almost too much for him.

"We'll find answers for your brother," he told her. "I promise."

That had been their objective from the start, and it was what Kai needed to focus on now also.

As Gage stepped out of the bathroom, Kai stood, thankful for the opening—the chance to get away.

"Am I good to get in the shower now?" he asked Tori. "With the stitches?"

"Yes, the bandage I put on your shoulder is

waterproof, but be careful with it anyway. Your stitches need to stay dry for one or two days."

"Will do." Her concern tugged at his heart, but Kai couldn't let himself be drawn toward her any further. "We can talk more in the morning."

Before she could say anything else, he walked away.

He'd found himself letting down his guard . . . and that was never a good idea.

WHEN TORI AWOKE the next morning, she forced herself to get out of bed, take a shower, and get dressed.

Her thoughts lingered on her conversation last night with Kai. His walls had gone up with so much force she'd nearly been knocked off her feet.

What had changed to cause that reaction? Had she said something that upset him?

She wasn't sure. But she'd been thinking about their talk all night, letting herself be bothered by it.

By the time she wandered into the living room, Kai was already drinking some coffee and studying Nathan's notes again.

He murmured good morning to her before excusing himself to get ready. Was he avoiding her? That was definitely how it seemed.

She grabbed a cup and put a pod into the Keurig so she could have some coffee also. Then she waited for it to brew, trying not to think too much about Kai's standoffishness.

Logically, she knew it was better if they kept their distance. The last thing she needed to think about at a time like this was romance. The truth was that falling in love hadn't been anything she'd *intended* on thinking about.

She hadn't expected to have feelings for Kai. They'd surprised her just as much as they might surprise anyone.

For a brief moment yesterday, she'd thought he shared those feelings. But apparently, she'd been wrong.

Perhaps she'd misinterpreted adrenaline and danger for chemistry.

Either way, Tori couldn't deny being disappointed.

But that didn't matter. Right now, she needed to concentrate on survival.

Where did they even go from here in order to find answers?

They had men chasing them. Pacemakers that could kill both Kai and Gage instantly. Many valid questions they still needed answers to.

How would they find those answers?

Off the top of her head, there were two things she wanted to do. The first was talking to the coroner. The second was figuring out who Howard Monarch was.

"You guys . . ." Gage hurried into the living area. "I've got bad news."

She grabbed her cup of coffee, now finished brewing, and turned toward him. "What's going on?"

"Where's Kai?" Gage looked around. "He needs to hear this."

"He's in the bathroom. What's happening?"

He held up his phone where three grainy photos had been posted. "We're wanted for a break-in at the doctor's office . . . and murder."

"What?" Tori darted to her feet. "We didn't kill anyone!"

"I know." Gage slowly shook his head, his jaw tightening. "But that's not what the evidence shows."

Kai appeared from the bathroom, his face freshly shaven and clean clothes on. "What happened?"

"Someone managed to get pictures of us last night when we broke into the doctor's office." Gage paced. "The people chasing us must have had someone hiding in the bushes, waiting for us and taking photos so they could set us up. We're also wanted for murder."

Kai froze. "Who's dead?"

"Dr. Landon Jean-Pierre." Gage shook his head, still pacing. "The police were able to access the security camera footage from outside the doctor's house. It shows the three of us were there the night he was killed."

"But we weren't there!" Tori's voice rose with exclamation. "How is that possible?"

"When someone is good with technology, anything is possible." Kai rubbed his jaw before moving his hand to his neck. "Now we're going to be on everyone's radar. This is going to make finding answers a thousand times harder."

"But now we need to find answers more than ever." Tori's head still spun at the thought of it. She closed her eyes and threw her head back.

"Yes, we do—unless we want to go to jail."

Tori opened her eyes and slowly lowered her head until her gaze met Kai's. "So we either go to jail or these guys kill us first."

Kai nodded slowly, a grim expression on his face. "We need to figure out what to do. Now."

———

Kai's determination to find answers grew with every passing moment.

Whoever was behind this would not get away with it. He promised himself that.

He pulled his hat down low as he, Gage, and Tori headed down the road.

Gage had gone to the store again and bought hats, sunglasses, etc.—typical disguises—for everyone so they could change their appearance.

They couldn't risk being caught.

That meant they couldn't stay at this motel again. Even though only Gage had checked them in last night, there was still a chance someone might recognize them. News that they were wanted would soon begin to spread, and more people would notice them.

Another agent, Trevor McGrath, had driven down from Ohio, where he'd just finished an assignment, so they could trade vehicles. Gage had handled the exchange earlier.

Everything equaled one big mess.

Twenty minutes later, they pulled to a stop in front of Thomas Morris's brick, colonial-style home. He was the medical examiner who'd handled Nathan's death.

They needed to talk to him and see what they could find out.

Kai glanced at her in the back seat. "You ready?"

Tori nodded, apprehension in her gaze. "Yes, I am."

It was Saturday, so they were counting on the man being home.

They were just far enough away from the city that

people in this area might not have seen the Atlanta news and wouldn't recognize their faces. That was Kai's hope, at least.

As per usual, Gage would wait in the car. Having all three of them go to the door would appear too intimidating and likely cause Dr. Morris to shut down.

Kai prayed this worked, and they were able to find some answers. The sooner they knew the truth, the quicker he could put distance between himself and Tori.

Was that what he wanted to do?

No.

But it was what he needed to do—for both their sakes.

Being around her was so hard when all he wanted to do was finish their conversation from last night. He should explain to her why he needed to keep his distance, how it was ultimately in her best interest. But he hadn't found the right time yet.

With Tori beside him, he rang the doorbell.

Kai stole a glance at her as they waited. She still looked apprehensive. But he couldn't blame her for that. This was a lot—even for him.

"You've got this," he murmured.

She nodded stiffly. "I hope so."

The door opened, and Dr. Morris stood there, staring at them with a wary look in his eyes.

"Sir," Kai started. "Sorry to drop by unannounced, but we were hoping to have a moment of your time."

Then he waited for the man's response.

CHAPTER
THIRTY

TORI TRIED to push down the wave of nerves she felt as she stared at Thomas Morris.

She'd seen a picture of the man online. But in real life, he looked larger—probably six foot five—with broad shoulders and a rounded belly. He was probably in his late fifties, with short salt-and-pepper hair accentuated with a receding hairline.

Even though it was September and still fairly warm, he wore a sweater vest as he stared at them. "If you're selling something, I'm not interested."

Tori broke out of her stupor and held up her hand before he could totally dismiss them. "Wait. We're not selling anything."

She knew there were many ways they could approach this. More aggressive styles or more civilized ones.

She, of course, wanted to go the more civilized route.

Dr. Morris paused with his hand on the door, a sure indication that he was prepared to close it in their face at his whim.

"I'm here about Nathan Bristow," she announced.

He squinted. "Who is Nathan Bristow?"

"He died of a cardiac arrest two weeks ago, and you did the examination," Tori reminded him.

An unreadable emotion flitted through his eyes, and he stepped back. "Those findings are confidential. And I especially don't appreciate people showing up at my house uninvited to try to discuss my work."

He started to shut the door, and Kai extended his leg. His foot blocked it.

Based on the scowl Dr. Morris gave Kai's foot, he didn't appreciate the move.

"We've traveled a long way, and we really need to speak with you," Kai said.

Now, more than anything, Tori wanted to talk to Dr. Morris. The fact he'd even remembered examining Nathan told her something. He probably dealt with hundreds of bodies every year—not just murders but natural deaths and suicides as well.

But he'd recognized Nathan's cause of death. That had to mean something.

"As I said before, autopsy results are not something I can discuss—" Dr. Morris started.

"You can discuss them with me. My name is Tori Bristow." She held her breath as she waited for the doctor's reaction. "Nathan Bristow was my brother."

Kai watched Dr. Morris, trying to anticipate his next move.

Part of Kai feared that as soon as he moved his foot, the doctor would slam the door and lock it, refusing to speak with them.

Kai stared at Dr. Morris as he waited to see if the doctor would do this the easy way or the hard way.

Finally, Dr. Morris released the door from his grip and took a slight step back. "I'll give you five minutes."

"Thank you." Kai slowly removed his foot.

Dr. Morris opened the door wider and invited them inside. But Kai watched as the man glanced outside, almost as if looking to see if anyone was nearby.

Had someone been watching him lately?

Dr. Morris pointed to a formal living area, and Kai and Tori sat on a stiff leather couch. The man didn't bother to offer any drinks, which was fine.

"What do you want to know?" Dr. Morris sat rigidly in a chair across from them.

Kai glanced at Tori, giving her the chance to take the lead. She was the one who'd started this investigation and the one who'd lost her brother.

She cleared her throat before starting. "Something about my brother's death never rang true to me. So I began doing my own investigation into what might have happened to him. And I don't believe he died of natural causes."

Dr. Morris's expression remained stoic. "What *do* you think?"

"I think that, for some reason, you fudged the results of the autopsy. I believe my brother had a pacemaker near his heart that caused it to stop beating."

"You're accusing me of altering the results of the autopsy?" Offense stretched through Dr. Morris's voice.

"Someone did," Tori told him honestly. "And I'm starting with you."

"Why in the world would I fudge the autopsy results?" He might as well have rolled his eyes the way he said the words with such disdain.

Tori exchanged a glance with Kai, who gave her a nod of encouragement. "I'm not sure exactly why. Maybe you were paid off. Maybe you were threatened. Maybe you didn't do it at all, but maybe after you turned in the report someone you work with did it. That's what I need to know."

Kai held his breath as he waited to see what the man would say this time.

Would Dr. Morris continue to deny what had happened? Would he kick them out? Call the police?

Kai prayed they'd finally get some answers . . . for Tori's sake.

TORI WATCHED the medical examiner's face.

Dr. Morris knew something. But would he share?

Finally, he said, "You shouldn't be looking into this."

Her heart pounded harder. That was all the confirmation she needed to prove there was some type of cover-up going on.

"I can't let this drop," she told him. "This is my brother we're talking about. He deserves justice."

Dr. Morris tugged at the collar of his shirt. "I only did what I was told."

"Who told you to do what?" Kai kept his voice even and calm, but his shoulders bristled.

"The orders came from above me, and they were very specific." He tugged his collar again, almost as if he were hot.

His house was freezing cold, however.

"Tell us more." Kai's gaze locked on the man.

Tori knew enough to know Kai was using his nice tone and that he'd get more aggressive if Dr. Morris didn't cooperate.

Dr. Morris let out a long, slow breath. He blinked several times. Let out another breath.

Finally, he said, "When I went to do the examination of Mr. Bristow, one of the first things I noticed was he had some type of device near his heart, similar to a pacemaker. But when I looked at his medical history, I didn't see any mentions of that. I also found a chip in his shoulder that I found perplexing."

"You reported that his death was due to cardiac arrest. Do you believe this pacemaker-like device is what ultimately killed him?" Tori could hardly breathe as she waited for his response.

"I do." He nodded slowly, clearly still cautious about how much he said. "It's possible that someone remotely controlled the device and decided to end his life."

"And the chip embedded in his shoulder?" Kai asked.

"If I had to guess, I'd say it was some type of tracking device."

Tori's thoughts continued to race. "What about his brain? Did you see anything unusual there?"

Dr. Morris shook his head. "I did not."

"Do you still have the devices?" Tori asked.

"Someone from the government picked them up. It was all very hush-hush."

"You didn't question it when these orders were given?" Kai continued to press.

"I was told that this man was a part of a highly classified government program, and that's why he had that kind of hardware in him," Dr. Morris said. "I was instructed not to mention the devices. That's why the results look the way they do. If I didn't change the official paperwork, someone above me would have."

Tori couldn't argue with his statement. She could see where it would be true.

"What about the tox screen?" she asked instead.

"It came back clear. That part of the report was true."

Kai leaned closer, his voice hardening. "So you have no idea who gave your boss these orders?"

"All I know is that it came from someone above us. Someone who wanted to keep Bristow's cause of death—and those implanted devices—a secret."

"And morally you didn't have a problem with that?" Tori didn't bother to keep the outrage from her voice. "You lied."

"I *did* have a problem with it. But I'm only a year away from retiring. So I decided to keep my mouth shut and to keep myself in check. Because the truth is, ever since I did that autopsy, I've noticed someone tailing me. And I've wondered if I'll even live to see retirement."

"We need to go now," Kai told Gage when they were back in the SUV. "Dr. Morris said someone has been watching him. We don't want to be made."

Gage sped away from the house. As he did, Kai's thoughts replayed the conversation multiple times. Each time, he felt even more angry.

Two blocks later, Gage asked, "Well? How did it go?"

They updated him on what the doctor had said.

Gage let out a whistle before his jaw hardened. "The more I hear, the less I like it."

"You and me both," Kai said. "Something's definitely going on here. Whatever it is, the person behind it is high-ranking."

"All this time I was thinking that someone on the outside was calling the shots for this." Tori leaned closer from the back seat. "Now it sounds like it's someone on the inside, someone who maybe works for the government . . . someone who's supposed to be one of the good guys."

"Do you think Larchmont could still pull these kinds of strings?" Kai asked Gage.

"There's no telling what that man is capable of." Gage's eyes narrowed. "I say we remain open to all the possibilities right now until we have more information. The one thing that's certain is that if we were to go to someone above Dr. Morris, I'm sure they would deny any knowledge of this. It might even end up getting another person killed."

"I tend to agree with you." Kai crossed his arms.

Tori let out a sigh beside him. "So where does this leave us?"

"I'm still curious about this Howard guy," Kai said. "That car that was following us is registered to him."

"Could it have been stolen?" Gage asked.

"I checked," Kai said. "It wasn't reported as stolen. I don't know how he connects with everything that's going on. In fact, I'd never heard of him until yesterday. But he could have some of the answers we need."

"Shouldn't we track him down then?" Tori asked.

"We probably should," Kai said. "We'll just need to be careful."

He scanned everything around them one more time.

He didn't see anyone suspicious. Now that those

chips were gone from him and Gage, maybe the bad guys wouldn't catch up with them again.

But he couldn't afford to let down his guard.

That was probably what these guys were counting on.

These men were still looking for Kai, Gage, and Tori. When they were located again, these men would strike.

When that happened, the three of them would need to be ready.

TORI HEARD a mental timer ticking in her head. The only problem was she didn't know when it would ding and this would all be over.

But she, Kai, and Gage couldn't go on like this forever.

Especially since the people they were chasing for answers seemed to be determined to either put them behind bars for a murder they didn't commit or to silence them for good.

They drove back toward the city. As they did, Tori kept her eyes wide open, not just for any signs of a dark sedan that might be following them. But also for any cops.

Going back to Atlanta was risky. She knew that. Their faces were no doubt plastered everywhere since they were wanted now in connection to Landon's murder.

Every time she thought of it, tension squeezed her heart.

She would never do anything to hurt Landon—would never do anything to hurt anyone.

But now Landon was dead, and Tori was a suspect in his death.

Even once this was over—if they survived—how would she bounce back from something like this?

She wasn't sure. She wasn't sure if this would have a truly happy ending or not.

They pulled into a parking garage several minutes later, and Gage cut the engine.

"Broadreach is located in the building across the street." Gage nodded to a high-rise. "I don't exactly know how we're going to do this. It's not like anyone's going to let us walk right up to Howard Monarch and ask questions. My guess is as high-powered as he is, he'll have multiple layers of security."

"So what's our plan?" Tori scooted closer to better hear the conversation.

"We could wait here and watch for him," Gage said. "When Mr. Monarch leaves, we could confront him. If that doesn't work, we could follow him. See where he lives. I couldn't find his address online. It might be better to corner him at home. Or maybe even if he goes out for dinner or something."

"That plan sounds a little flimsy." Kai frowned. "I'm not sure how effective it's going to be. It leaves too much to chance."

"You have a better idea?" Gage glanced at his colleague, his eyebrows raised.

Kai's frown deepened. "Unfortunately, I don't. You're right that we're just going to have to be patient and wait for the right opportunity. Even if this Howard guy is guilty, it's not as if he's going to own up to anything just because we ask him."

"Do we stick together?" Tori asked. "Or are we more likely to be noticed if we do that?"

"We're definitely more likely to be noticed if all three of us are together," Kai said. "But we can't afford to leave you alone either. I think we have a good view of his building from here. We can stay in the 4Runner and wait."

His words brought her a measure of relief. She didn't want to be alone.

She knew what that end result would probably be —she'd most likely end up dead.

"So we hang out here until we see him?" she clarified.

"Yes, that's the plan." Gage leaned back in his seat. "For now."

Tori's heart thumped harder into her rib cage. She

didn't even want to think about what could go wrong in the meantime.

She could do this. She *had* to do this.

For Nathan's sake.

———

Kai was not only waiting for Howard to emerge, but he was also keeping his eyes open for both the police and for the men who'd been following them.

Too much was on the line.

He glanced in the back seat at Tori, and regret filled him.

They'd had a moment last night. He couldn't deny that they had.

But he'd had no choice but to pull away—for her sake.

He wasn't in a place for a relationship. Larchmont had made sure of that.

However . . . Gage, Austin, and Trevor were now in successful relationships. They'd struggled with many of the same things that Kai now struggled with, and they'd overcome them.

Maybe Kai could do the same.

This, however, was the worst time to figure that out. Kai had too many other pressing things he needed to focus on.

They'd been sitting in the SUV two hours when someone leaving the building caught his eye.

"Is that him?" Kai asked.

Gage and Tori both straightened, and their gazes followed where he was pointing.

Sure enough, Howard was leaving. Two men flanked either side of him.

"What do you think?" Gage asked. "Should we approach him? Or follow him?"

"I doubt he'll talk." Kai tapped the side of the door with his finger as he thought it through.

"We may not have another opportunity," Tori reminded them. "He may be unreachable once he gets to his house."

Kai couldn't argue with that.

"Okay," Kai murmured. "Let's go see what he says when we catch him by surprise."

CHAPTER
THIRTY-THREE

A RUSH of nerves fluttered through Tori.

She had no idea how this would turn out. But she knew the confrontation was worth a shot.

This man could have the information they needed.

"Stay close," Kai called over his shoulder as he and Gage took the lead.

He didn't have to worry about that. Tori didn't plan on going anywhere.

They strode across the street toward Howard as he headed toward an SUV.

"Excuse me!" Kai called. "Can we have a word with you?"

As soon as Kai spoke, Howard's guards moved in front of the man. One quickly shoved him in the SUV while the other stalked toward Kai, Gage, and Tori.

"Stay back," the guard told them.

"We just want to talk." Kai paused as if hoping to get through to him.

"Then make an appointment."

"He won't speak with us," Kai continued.

Tori knew they hadn't actually tried to speak with the man. But she had no doubt Kai's words were true. There was no way Howard would agree to talk to them.

"Then I don't know what to tell you. But speaking to Mr. Monarch without invitation isn't acceptable. Now, if you'll excuse me—" The guard started to step toward the SUV.

"Why are you having men follow us?" Tori called, wanting Howard to hear the question before he left.

He glanced at her from inside his SUV, his eyes narrow.

He *had* heard her.

Would he answer?

She waited. But he slowly turned his head away from them, blatantly ignoring them.

"That's enough." The guard raised his wrist to his mouth and muttered something into his watch. Then he extended his hand and said, "Back away."

They stayed back.

With one last glance at them, the guard climbed into the SUV beside Howard, and the vehicle took off.

Tori, Kai, and Gage glanced at each other.

Without making a scene—which was the last thing they wanted—that was all they could do.

How were they going to break through to this guy and find out answers?

———

Kai's jaw tightened.

That hadn't gone the way he'd hoped.

Now Howard would probably put out an alert on them to ensure they never came close again. Short of breaking into his house to talk to him . . .

Kai frowned. Breaking in *was* a possibility, he supposed. But it was extreme, and it should be a last resort.

If they were caught, the police would *really* have a reason to arrest them.

"Let's get back to the SUV." Gage nodded toward the parking garage across the street. "We're too exposed out here."

"I agree." Kai placed his hand on Tori's back and guided her to the SUV.

Thankfully, no one seemed to be looking their way.

But that man was untouchable, Kai continued to muse. Why?

There was more to this. There had to be.

Whenever he'd worked high-security assignments with protective detail like that, there had always been a good reason.

They hurried into the parking garage and up the stairs.

But just as their SUV came into sight, so did the man standing in front of it.

"It's him," Tori muttered, her steps slowing. "The man who approached me at Alfie's apartment."

Kai bristled, and he jutted out his arm to stop her from walking any farther. "Stand out of the way over there."

Tori scooted back.

Then Kai and Gage stormed toward the man, ready to find out some answers.

CHAPTER
THIRTY-FOUR

TORI BACKED up until her legs hit another car.

She froze, her adrenaline pumping.

She couldn't believe this man was here. That he'd found them.

Now what would happen?

She could hardly breathe as she watched Kai and Gage approach the guy.

What if the man pulled a gun? What if something happened to Kai and Gage?

The man threw the first punch at Gage, who ducked.

The man immediately came at Gage again.

Tori could hardly keep straight who threw punches at the other. The fight was a jumble of bodies, limbs, and fists.

Yet she couldn't look away either.

Dear Lord, please . . . help them.

The men all paused a moment, catching their breath as they stared off at each other.

Then Kai charged toward the man. His shoulder hit the guy's abdomen.

Kai knocked the wind out of the man as they collided with the SUV.

Then he pinned the man in place.

Go, Kai . . .

But it was too early to cheer. Things could still go south.

"Who are you?" Kai demanded, his nostrils flaring.

"It doesn't matter who I am," the man said with a grunt.

"What do you want from us?" Gage crowded the man from the other side.

"You need to back off." Veins bulged at the man's temples.

"And if we don't?" Gage asked.

"Then it's our job to stop you."

Kai held him down with his gaze. "Who do you work for?"

"It's not important."

"I say it is." Kai cocked his head.

Gaining a burst of strength, the man shoved off the SUV and charged at him again.

Tori held her breath as she waited to see what would happen next.

—————

Kai decided to try a different approach.

He nodded at Gage.

Then they both grabbed the man and pinned him again, this time against a concrete pillar.

Had this guy really thought he could take both of them?

The fact was the man *had* put up a good fight. He was well trained, his techniques similar to those Kai and Gage had been taught. Coincidence?

He was about to find out.

"I don't want to hurt you," Kai told the man through gritted teeth. "I think you and I are on the same team."

"You don't know what you're talking about," he muttered.

"But I do," Kai continued. "You went through Project Elevate, didn't you? Only maybe it was called a different name when you participated in the program."

Something flashed through the man's eyes before quickly disappearing. "I don't know what you're talking about," he repeated.

"Let me guess—you don't have any close family.

Maybe you even grew up in foster care. You joined the military right after high school and were chosen for a special program."

The muscles across the man's chest tightened. "You know nothing about me. *Nothing*!"

"You know it's true," Kai said. "You thought you and your guys were the only ones out there. You had no idea there were others who'd been trained in the same way. That's what we thought too. Now we know we're like puppets doing someone else's bidding."

The man said nothing.

Maybe Kai was finally getting through to him.

"Did you know there's a pacemaker implanted near your heart?" Kai asked him. "That if the person pulling the strings decides to hit a button one day, you'll drop dead? Just like Tori's brother, Nathan?"

The man glanced at Tori. His expression softened a moment. "You're Nathan's sister?"

"I am." She offered a curt nod and no other information.

His eyes widened.

"I thought his death was suspicious." The guy glanced around. "You guys are telling the truth?"

"We are," Kai told him.

The man remained silent a moment before nodding. "We should talk. But not here."

"Why not here?" Kai asked. "Why not now?"

The man glanced around again. "In case someone is watching. We're too exposed."

As if perfectly timed, two people exited the stairway and walked to their cars.

Kai released his grip on the man but remained close—just in case.

"Where?" Gage asked.

The man rattled off a location and time.

This could be a trap, Kai realized. Letting this guy go could be a huge mistake.

But Kai thought he saw sincere curiosity in the man's eyes.

Maybe if they could talk, they could make sense of what was going on.

Kai hesitated only another second before stepping back.

He prayed he'd made the right choice.

If not . . . he didn't even want to consider the repercussions.

CHAPTER
THIRTY-FIVE

TORI WATCHED the man walk away, her heart pounding in her ears.

Was this a mistake?

Only once the man had disappeared from sight did Kai usher her into the SUV. Meanwhile, Gage checked beneath the vehicle.

What was he looking for? A tracking device? Or maybe something even worse—something like a bomb?

The blood drained from her face.

She was in over her head. She had been ever since she started looking into her brother's death.

Finally, Gage climbed in the SUV, slammed the door, and they took off.

"Are you guys really going to meet this guy tonight?" Tori had overheard that much and now she was desperate to know what Kai and Gage were thinking.

Did they have some type of plan she didn't know about? Some type of tactic that would keep them safe? The whole thing sounded too risky.

"We need to meet him," Kai said. "See what he knows. Maybe we can help each other out."

"But what if it's a setup?" Her voice cracked as she asked the question. "What if you're ambushed?"

"We know that's a risk," Kai said, his voice mellow and serious.

On one hand, it made her feel better to know Kai and Gage were aware of what they might get into.

On the other hand, what if this ended up getting them killed?

For a split second, Tori wished she'd never tried to find Kai. That she hadn't come to him with this information. That she hadn't asked so many questions.

Then maybe Landon would still be alive. Maybe attempts wouldn't have been made on Kai's life. On Gage's life. On her own life.

Yet how could she turn a blind eye to everything she knew?

She couldn't.

The thought settled heavy across her chest, making it hard to breathe.

Gage pulled from the parking garage and onto

the city street. Tori wasn't even sure where they were heading. She didn't ask.

She had no doubt Kai and Gage had a plan. She would go where they took her.

She did know, however, that they still had four hours before they were supposed to meet this guy.

Four hours was enough time for trouble to find them again.

At that thought, she glanced out the window beside her as Gage stopped at a red light.

A cop car pulled up beside them.

The officer in the passenger seat glanced over and did a double take at them.

Her gut clenched.

"You guys." Her voice shook. "I think we might have a problem."

———

Kai saw the cop punching something into his computer.

Tension instantly threaded through him.

"They're going to be onto us," he told Gage. "We need to move."

As soon as the light turned and the car in front of him moved forward, Gage accelerated and took the first right turn.

Kai glanced in the mirror.

The police car followed in the same direction.

They'd been made. He was sure of it.

He and Gage were going to need to make a quick decision on how to handle this situation before things turned ugly.

The police car's sirens yelped twice, the quick bursts of sound indicating they should pull over.

"What's our move?" Kai asked Gage.

"If we let them pull us over then we're all going to jail. Knowing the people behind this, they're going to fudge more evidence and make it look as if we're guilty. We can't take that chance, especially not when we're so close to finding answers."

As soon as the words left Gage's lips, he jerked the wheel and made another righthand turn. They were almost out of the downtown area.

The last thing that Kai wanted was a police chase through these streets.

But that was exactly what it appeared they were going to get.

The police siren chirped again, giving them one last warning.

Gage hit the accelerator, and they flew through a red light, barely missing several oncoming vehicles. Horns blared from every direction.

"I hope you know what you're doing," Tori said in the back seat, her voice trembling.

If there was one thing he and Gage were good at doing, it was losing people.

But the traffic and congestion would make it difficult right now.

Gage ran through the next light, and more vehicles slammed on their brakes.

The police car zoomed behind them, sirens now blazing and lights flashing.

It was just a matter of time before more police joined the chase. Kai had no doubt the driver had already put out an APB.

This wouldn't be an easy situation to maneuver.

Unfortunately, they had no other choice but to keep trying.

CHAPTER
THIRTY-SIX

TORI SQUEEZED HER EYES SHUT.

She didn't like any of this.

Yet at the same time, she knew they couldn't simply pull over either.

Please, God. I know this seems like such a selfish prayer. But if you could let us get away . . . let us catch a break. Please!

Guilt filled her as she realized what she was praying. She prayed they'd be able to break the law and get away with it.

But considering these circumstances and the injustice they were fighting, she hoped maybe God would understand.

Gage made another sharp turn, followed by another. More brakes squealed and people laid on their horns.

But they kept moving forward.

Tori had no idea how they were going to get away with this.

Her eyes popped open as she felt movement beside her. Kai climbed into the back seat—and then kept going into the back cargo area.

"What are you doing?" she murmured.

"You'll see," he said. "Or maybe it's better if you don't see."

She couldn't seem to close her eyes or look away. Instead, she watched as he fiddled with a compartment in the floor.

Tori squinted as Kai pulled something from the carpeted area—some type of long chain with spikes on it.

A few seconds later, Kai cracked open the back of the trunk, just enough for her to hear the wind.

He wasn't going to jump out, was he?

No, instead he dropped the chain from the small opening.

Tori's breath caught when she heard a popping sound.

She sucked in a breath.

What had he just done?

———

Kai watched as the cop car behind him swerved.

Its tires had run over the spike strip.

Now the vehicle bumped to a stop.

Another police car, the one directly behind the first, apparently didn't see what happened. That officer also hit the strip.

The tires went flat, and they lurched to a stop.

That would hold the police off, at least for a while.

Kai climbed back into the front seat.

Meanwhile, Gage didn't slow down.

In fact, as they reached the warehouse district, Gage darted behind some buildings and threw the SUV in Park.

"You don't think they're going to find us back here?" Tori's voice lilted with apprehension.

"We have a plan for that also." Gage nodded at Kai.

Kai jumped from the front seat and hurried to the back, walking around this time.

He opened another bag—with license plates in it.

Working quickly, he switched the plates. Then he added a couple of magnetic stickers to throw off the police's scent. They all also switched hats and shirts.

Then Kai climbed back in the SUV, and Gage eased back onto the road.

"You think this is going to work?" Tension captured Tori's voice.

"It has before," Kai told her. "This should allow

us at least to get out of town. The police will be looking for the make of our vehicle, but there are many like this on the road. We should have just bought ourselves some time."

As they headed down the street, Kai angled his gaze behind him and saw two cop cars zoom past, their cars perpendicular to their route.

It looked as if their plan may have worked.

But they were so far from being able to let their guard down and relax.

No, they still had entirely too much on the line to do that.

TORI COULDN'T BELIEVE that plan had worked, but she wasn't complaining.

She, Kai, and Gage traveled away from the city—Kai staying low in his seat so it would only look like one person was up front.

Occasionally, Tori spotted a cop car in the distance. But no one seemed to recognize them.

They'd had so many close calls.

Once her lungs loosened enough, she finally asked, "Where are we going now?"

"We need to find a place to lie low," Gage said. "And we'll need to grab something to eat so we can keep our energy up. We still have a few hours until we meet this guy—if he really shows."

"Isn't it too risky to go to any type of hotel?" she asked.

"We'll find a dumpy one," Kai said. "And we'll pay in cash."

Twenty minutes later, they pulled up to a beige and brown motel located in a rundown area of town.

Not ideal accommodations, but it would have to do.

Kai went to reserve a room. Then, once he had a key in hand, they all went inside their temporary second-story accommodation. Six other vehicles were parked outside the building, indicating the place wasn't full, but there were other people staying here.

Tori paused inside the room. The orange-and-brown bedspreads and nasty-looking brown carpet didn't do anything to set her mind at ease.

But at least they should be out of sight. For now. That was the important thing.

She sat on the edge of the bed, probably a little too hard. But everything they'd been through was catching up with her.

She was tired. Now that she thought about it, she was hungry also.

Gage seemed to read her mind. "There's a Taco Bell across the street. I can run in there and get us some food and bring it back. Sound good?"

"Sounds perfect," Tori said.

He left a moment later, leaving her and Kai alone.

Tori glanced at Kai, who stood near the window,

and frowned. He looked as if he'd aged since she had met him only a few days ago. His eyes looked tired and his body on edge.

She knew his awareness that a device inside him had the potential to kill him at any moment had taken its toll.

"I'm sorry I pulled you into all this," she said quietly.

He dropped the curtain and turned toward her. "You didn't pull us into anything. We were a part of it long before you brought it to our attention. It's better that we know."

He rubbed his hand across his chest near his heart, as Tori had caught him doing several times since the discovery of the pacemaker was made.

"I wish I could do something in order to help you," she said. "But I'm definitely no heart surgeon."

That got a small smile out of him. "I could see where this would require a specialty skill. The truth of the matter is, I'm not sure who I trust to get this thing out of me. The only way I'm going to believe it's really gone is if you're in the room while the surgery is taking place, and you see it happen."

Tori was honored he trusted her that much.

Despite the weirdness between them yesterday, maybe things weren't as strained as she'd initially thought.

***

Gage returned several minutes later with a bag full of food and a drink carrier with three large fountain drinks that he set on the table. "I didn't know what anyone wanted so I got a bit of everything. Dig in."

Kai reached into the bag and grabbed the first thing his fingers hit. A beef chalupa.

That would work.

Tori was daintier as she peered in the bag and grabbed a soft taco. Even though she'd said she was hungry, she couldn't prove it with the way she ate right now, taking slow, small bites.

Her gaze looked heavy and distracted.

They were mostly quiet as they ate, each lost in their own thoughts.

Meeting this guy tonight was risky. They all knew it. Anticipated it.

After they finished eating, Gage began calling their colleagues to tell them what was going on. While he did that, Kai tried to do some research into this man they were meeting.

Everything had happened so fast that Kai hadn't had a chance to get a picture of the man, nor did he know his name.

He found nothing online, which didn't surprise him. He didn't have enough to go on.

Finally, Kai stood.

They knew what it was time for.

If they were going to meet this guy, they needed to get ready to go.

Kai just prayed they didn't regret this.

TORI LISTENED as Kai and Gage discussed what to do with her during tonight's meeting.

They talked as if she wasn't in the room. Apparently, leaving her in the hotel was risky. But so was taking her with them.

After they debated for several minutes, she stepped closer, tired of being quiet. "I want to go."

The two men stopped talking and stared at her.

"It could be dangerous," Kai said. "We don't know what we're getting ourselves into."

"I know," she told them. "I'm prepared to take that risk. I definitely don't want to stay here."

Finally, Gage nodded. "Okay, but if we tell you to stay put, then you've got to promise to listen."

"I will."

"Since that's settled . . ." Kai rose. "We need to go."

Tori felt the tension in the air as they headed back to the SUV. Everything outside appeared normal. She'd halfway expected the police to have found them, to just be waiting to pounce.

But the cops hadn't located them. Not yet.

The ride to their meeting spot was quiet except for Kai and Gage occasionally discussing various tactics.

She glanced out the window. Darkness had fallen outside, and she shivered at the sight of it.

Would they walk away from this meeting? Even if they did, would they be the same afterward?

She had no idea what this guy's agenda was. To help them? Or to covertly destroy them?

Dear Lord . . . please be with us. Please!

Her palms were sweaty.

But all Tori could do for the rest of the ride was continue to pray.

———

Apprehension rippled through Kai as they headed toward the warehouse. Before they reached it, Gage's phone rang.

Larchmont's number popped on the screen.

"Should we answer?" Gage asked.

"Probably," Kai muttered with a frown.

Gage put their boss on speaker. Before he even said hello, Larchmont lit into them. "You two are wanted for murder? Do you even realize the repercussions of this?"

Gage cast Kai a look. "We're well aware."

"What were you thinking? This is not the case I assigned you to."

"Something popped up that we needed to look into," Kai said.

"You're supposed to be in DC." Anger zinged through his voice.

"Listen, we can't talk right now," Gage said.

"You'll talk when I say you talk—"

"We'll call you later," Gage rushed.

Before Larchmont said anything else, Gage ended the call.

A moment of silence fell in the SUV.

Kai let out a sigh. "Larchmont was the last person I wanted to talk to."

"You and me both." Gage let out a half-snort at the words.

"You think he knows?"

Gage rubbed his jaw, his tone heavy as he said, "It wouldn't surprise me. But we can't worry about that now."

They pulled up to the warehouse where they were supposed to meet.

On one hand, this location was a good idea because most likely no one would catch them out here. But on the other hand, if anything were to happen to them, no one would find them for days.

Meeting this guy here was a gamble. But Kai hoped the risk would be worth the reward.

Gage pulled to a stop in the shadows. As he cut the engine, he glanced at Kai. "We're right on time. Do you think this guy is here?"

"We're about to find out." Kai glanced back at Tori. "You should stay here with the doors locked. We don't know what we are up against right now."

"I figured that much," she murmured with a resigned frown.

His gaze lingered on her another moment.

There were things he'd like to say. Things he knew would be a bad idea to express aloud.

How was it possible to begin to care about someone in such a short amount of time? It didn't make any sense. Nor was it wise.

That thought settled on him like a weight.

Kai pulled his gaze away from Tori and opened his door.

He waited until he heard the lock click behind him before walking away.

Then he and Gage headed toward a stretch of pavement behind the building. A lone streetlight shone above them.

Best he could tell, no one was here.

But if this guy was as smart as Kai thought he might be, there was a good chance he *was* here, standing just out of sight.

Kai stood poised to grab his gun if necessary. He didn't like being out here in the open. It was risky.

And possibly calculated.

He had to consider every possibility as to how this would turn out.

"What if this guy doesn't show?" Gage scanned their surroundings.

"I think he will." The man had seemed sincerely surprised by the revelations they'd shared with him and had seemed like he wanted to know more.

Kai hoped his gut instincts didn't fail him now.

Tension zinged in the air as he and Gage anticipated what might happen.

Then Kai heard a footfall.

Was it him? The man they were waiting for?

Kai held his breath as he waited to see who it was.

CHAPTER
THIRTY-NINE

KAI WATCHED as a shadow stepped into the light.

It was him. The man they'd confronted earlier.

Kai watched with bated breath, halfway expecting more guys to be here.

But he only saw the man they'd arranged the meeting with.

The guy raised his hands as if to show he was unarmed.

Kai's shoulders relaxed—but just slightly.

The man stepped closer before pausing six or so feet away. "You came."

"*You* came," Gage echoed. "We weren't sure what to think."

"I wanted to talk to you, but I had to make sure I wasn't followed. That's why I'm a little late."

The three of them stood assessing each other.

"My name is Stephen Garner," the man finally said.

Kai and Gage introduced themselves officially also.

Stephen's gaze remained cautious, his shoulders taut, as he stood in front of them. "Tell me what you know."

"Gage and I both went through Project Elevate," Kai started. "We thought our team was the only one, but we've discovered we're not. I believe you went through the program too."

Stephen's eyes widened as if he considered his response. Then he shrugged. "I don't know what you're talking about."

"I think you do." Kai's voice hardened.

Was this guy starting to play a game now? Why the change of heart?

Kai's guard went up. "We're all in the same boat. The military used us as Frankensteins, experimenting on us to develop the perfect soldier."

Stephen remained quiet.

"You might as well stop denying it." Gage's voice sounded no-nonsense. "You wouldn't have come tonight if something about this didn't ring true."

Kai waited for Stephen to break and admit he knew what was going on.

Kai saw the wheels turning in the man's mind as

he tried to process what they were saying. As he tried to determine how to react.

Admitting he knew what Kai and Gage were talking about would open a whole new can of hypothetical worms. There would be no going back.

His life would change.

So would Kai's and Gage's.

"I wasn't aware there were more of us either," Stephen finally confessed.

Kai's lungs loosened at the admission. Maybe they would make some progress. "How many are there that you know of?"

"There were twelve on my team. You?"

"Twelve," Gage said. "When were you recruited?"

"When I was nineteen—fifteen years ago."

Kai's breath caught. Stephen was brought into this program before he was. Kai had only come on board ten years ago.

Maybe Stephen was first generation—or, at least, the generation before Kai and Gage. For all Kai knew, this could have been going on for decades. Nothing felt certain right now.

"Where did you train?" Kai needed more information in order to verify this was all true.

"Michigan. You?"

His jaw tightened when he heard the confirmation. "Same. How long have you been out? Did you leave on your own?"

"They told us the program was shut down, that they lost funding. We'd had a number of issues, including some of our guys acting erratically."

Erratically? He didn't like the sound of that.

"What happened to those guys?" Gage narrowed his eyes as he waited for the answer.

"They mysteriously disappeared. The rest of us were hired as para-military contractors—probably so the government could keep an eye on us."

The details sounded very similar to their own situation, only it had all been lies. So many lies.

What was the truth even?

"Who are you working for now?" Kai asked.

"A man who goes by the name Rafferty. He ran the military program I was a part of and then he recruited us to join him in his new ventures when he became a civilian. That's all I know about him. I've never actually seen him."

Rafferty? Nathan had mentioned him also.

"You've never seen this Rafferty guy?" Kai clarified. "Even though he was in charge of the military program and your current job?"

"He has people doing his work. He never makes appearances in person. I know it sounds weird. Believe me, we all think so also."

Interesting . . .

"Who hired you to follow us?" Gage asked.

His gaze became shadowed. "I was told by my boss that I needed to act as protective detail to Howard Monarch. As perhaps you know also, I wasn't given much of an explanation nor did I expect one. I simply came to do my job."

"You followed us to that apartment complex," Kai said.

"I was told you were part of a possible plot against Mr. Monarch," Stephen explained. "I thought I could question you all, but then I realized that was a bad idea. That's when I left."

"What did your boss tell you about the assignment?" Kai asked.

"I was told he was being pursued by people who wanted to get their hands on the technology he's developed. I assumed that was you two." He paused. "So why are you going after him?"

"We believe he might be connected with the death of Nathan Bristow," Kai stated.

Stephen crossed his arms as if settling in for the rest of the conversation, a healthy dose of wariness in his gaze. "I was told Nathan died of a cardiac arrest."

"That's what we heard as well," Gage said. "But, as we mentioned earlier, we believe there's more to his death than meets the eye."

"I've been suspicious there's been something going on also," Stephen said. "But I've felt powerless to find out answers. Now that I know this . . . what am I supposed to do? What are *we* supposed to do?"

That was an excellent question.

———

Tori could hardly sit still. All she could think about was the parking lot meeting. What was being said? Revealed?

There hadn't been any type of physical altercation. The men appeared to be discussing things in a civilized manner. She praised God for that.

Now that she knew it was safe, part of her wanted to get out of the vehicle and join the conversation. After all, Nathan had been her brother, and she'd been the one who'd set this investigation into action.

But she'd promised to stay put so she would—even if her curiosity was killing her.

As she leaned back in her seat, her gaze traveled to the men.

She squinted as she studied the man Kai and Gage met with. When she saw him the first time, she thought he looked familiar.

Was he one of Nathan's coworkers? Could that be right?

The more she thought about it, the more she thought it might be.

She'd seen Nathan talking to a man outside his house one evening. When she'd asked Nathan who, he'd said it was no big deal. That the man was one of his colleagues who had a question.

That had been this man, hadn't it?

She felt certain that was correct.

Her gaze traveled to another building behind the men.

She squinted.

Why had she thought she saw movement there? Was she seeing things?

Then she realized it was most likely the shadow of one of the men standing under the light.

Right? That was what it had to be.

She glanced back at Kai, Gage, and the stranger and saw they were still talking.

But familiar apprehension rose in her.

Her gaze swerved back to the area where she'd thought the shadows had moved.

There it was again. That same movement.

That same bad feeling brewed inside her.

Was it really a shadow? Or was there more to it?

Tori wished she knew. But the building was so far away, and it was so dark. It was almost impossible to know.

She couldn't pull her gaze away now. If Kai and Gage were in trouble, she needed to warn them.

She kept watching, waiting for another sign or a clearer view of what was happening.

She sucked in a breath when she saw more movement.

That was *not* a shadow from Kai or Gage.

Someone was lurking near the other building.

Someone dressed all in black.

She was certain of it.

Tori needed to warn Kai and Gage—now.

"LET ME GET THIS STRAIGHT." Stephen narrowed his eyes, not bothering to hide his skepticism. "You think the people in charge of this program have the power to kill us off by simply hitting a button?"

Kai could understand his hesitancy to believe them. The story did sound outlandish.

"We know how it sounds," Kai said. "But yes. Gage and I both had X-rays done. We both have some type of metal device implanted near our hearts. We also had chips in our shoulders that were most likely used for tracking."

Stephen stared at him a moment before shaking his head and taking a step back. "That sounds crazy."

"We thought so too until we saw it with our own eyes," Gage said.

Stephen touched his shoulder, rubbing it.

Realization slammed into Kai.

Kai and Gage had their GPS chips removed.

But Stephen had not.

And that meant . . .

Kai quickly glanced around.

Had anyone followed Stephen here?

As if to answer, gunfire split the air.

"Get down!" Kai yelled.

Stephen grunted as he grabbed his shoulder.

He'd been hit, hadn't he? Pain stretched across his face.

Kai drew his gun as he searched for the shooter.

More gunshots rang out.

They needed to get out of here. There was no place to take cover.

Kai looked up in time to see headlights headed toward them.

He prepared himself to shoot.

That was when he realized it was Gage's SUV.

Had someone done something to Tori?

Or was she driving straight toward them?

He needed to be certain what was going on.

———

Tori threw on the brakes and rolled down the window as she got closer to Kai and Gage.

"Get in!" she shouted.

Gage and Kai quickly climbed inside.

Then Kai grabbed Stephen and pulled him in also.

As she turned the SUV away from the shooters, the back window shattered.

These people—he was certain more than one was here—were still shooting.

Why did Tori have to be the one in the driver's seat? But there was no time for anyone to take her place.

"That way!" Gage shouted beside her as he pointed toward an alley.

She tugged on the wheel and turned between two more warehouses.

But she slammed on brakes when another vehicle appeared in front of her.

Instead, she threw the vehicle into Reverse. Then she jammed on the accelerator.

They began to rapidly back through the alley.

"Don't hit the wall!" Kai yelled, craning his neck back so he could see. "You're too close."

Tori gritted her teeth. She was doing her best here.

Yet she didn't dare breathe.

Not until she cleared the alley.

Once the buildings disappeared from either side of her, she finally released a sigh.

She'd gotten through that.

But there were more challenges to come.

She jerked the wheel again. There was nowhere to go on her right side. So she headed back left.

Toward the first shooter.

Not ideal, but she didn't have very much choice right now.

"Get down!" Gage yelled.

She ducked as low as possible in order not to be hit.

Despite that, the front glass shattered.

A scream escaped, but she continued gripping the wheel. Continued pressing the accelerator.

She had to get away from these guys. It was their only chance at survival.

When she sat up higher in her seat, she saw a gunman directly in front of them.

Her heart pounded in her ears.

If she didn't stop, she would hit him.

But if she did stop, then he would shoot them.

CHAPTER
FORTY-ONE

TORI CONTINUED TO BARREL FORWARD, even though she knew it could be a death wish.

But she didn't want to hit anyone either.

"Keep going!" Kai yelled.

Despite her hesitation, she charged straight ahead.

Straight toward the man.

Kai raised his head to watch and held his breath.

When she was only a few feet from hitting the man, he dove out of the way.

Just like Kai thought he might.

"Keep going," Kai told her. "You can do this."

He saw the apprehension in her tight shoulders. The white-knuckle grip on the steering wheel. Her wide eyes. The slight gleam of sweat across her forehead.

She continued pressing the accelerator. As they zoomed away from the warehouse area, Gage called out directions.

The wind hit them in the face, bringing a chill with it. Every once in a while, a stray speck of glass flew back and hit one of them.

They could deal with that much more easily than they could deal with being shot.

Speaking of which . . .

Kai glanced back at Stephen. "You okay?"

He touched his shoulder and grimaced. "I think so."

As Kai looked closer, he noticed the bullet hadn't just skimmed Stephen's arm. It had gone through his shoulder. Blood covered the man's shirt.

He grabbed a towel from the back and pressed it into his wound. "Hold this over it."

Stephen took the towel. "Where are we going?"

"That's a good question," Tori called over her shoulder. "Do we go back to the motel? Or is that too risky?"

"I say we get away from here and pull off onto the side of the road to check this wound out before we decide what to do next," Gage said. "We can't take any chances."

"Good call," Kai said.

Gage continued to give directions. A few minutes

later, they pulled to a stop on the side of a country road. So far, they hadn't been followed.

But they couldn't afford to let down their guard.

"Tori, this is Stephen. Stephen, Tori. She's a nurse." Gage introduced them.

They both nodded at each other.

"Tori, could you check out his shoulder?" Kai asked. "I know we're asking you to do a lot of things you never signed up for. But we don't have much of a choice right now."

She glanced at them in the rearview mirror again before nodding. "Of course."

She climbed out and walked to the door behind her, opening it. As she did, Kai shone his flashlight on Stephen's wound.

Tori cringed when she saw the gaping hole. "That one had to hurt."

"Just a little," Stephen said through gritted teeth.

"I'm going to need to see that shoulder."

Kai pulled a knife from his pocket and cut the sleeve from Stephen's arm to the collar.

He glanced at Tori as she stared at it. "What do you think?"

Tori frowned as she leaned closer to better examine the wound.

But Kai knew that taking Stephen to the hospital wasn't an option.

That was one of multiple reasons Kai prayed her news wasn't bad.

———

Tori looked at the wound and frowned. "It's rough, but it looks like the bullet hit right where the chip would have been. I don't see how it could still be there. However, Stephen's not in a position for me to dig around under his skin and confirm."

Kai nodded slowly, his emotions perfectly controlled. "Then we need you to make your best guess."

She stared at the wound another moment, nibbling on her bottom lip. Finally, she nodded. "My most educated guess is that the chip has been destroyed."

"Do you think you can clean up that wound?" Kai asked.

She flinched at the thought. "It's going to be painful. But the bullet went straight through. That's a good thing. Nothing needs to be dug out. I don't see where it hit any bones or anything."

"Good to know," Stephen said through gritted teeth.

"However, what I don't know is . . . if the bullet hit the chip . . . what if pieces of that chip are still inside him?" She frowned as she said the words.

"Will you be able to see that once you clean him up?" Kai narrowed his eyes as he seemed to think it through.

"Maybe," she answered honestly. "I'll see what I can do back at the motel. We still have the first aid kit so I can use that." She glanced up at him, still not knowing what had transpired in the conversation. "Can we trust him?"

Kai nodded from behind Stephen. "We can."

She hoped Kai was right. He had better instincts about these things than she did.

But her nerves were still on edge.

"Gage, please say you're going to drive now." She glanced at him, her gaze pleading.

"Absolutely," he answered.

She released the breath she hadn't even realized she'd been holding. Then she climbed into the passenger seat.

They would get back to the motel, and she would clean this stranger up.

Then Kai and Gage would hopefully share more about what they'd learned.

KAI WATCHED as Gage parked behind the motel. Anyone who saw the SUV with its busted windows and bullet holes would become suspicious, and they couldn't risk that.

Nor would they be able to safely drive the vehicle tomorrow without raising attention.

They would need to figure out a new plan.

But first, they needed to treat Stephen's wound. Even though the bullet had managed to avoid anything major, the wound still needed to be cleaned and treated before infection could set in.

Kai's best guess was that someone had tracked Stephen to their meeting tonight and then ambushed them. Based on the expression on Stephen's face, he'd had no idea the attack would take place. Plus, the fact he'd been shot made it seem unlikely he was a part of what had unfolded.

Kai hoped their theory was right and any type of tracking device that might have been inside Stephen had been destroyed by the bullet.

They all climbed out, and Kai and Gage glanced around to make sure no one was nearby watching.

Everything appeared clear.

They followed Kai up the stairs to their room on the second floor.

Seconds before he used his keycard to unlock the door, the hair on the back of his neck rose.

What had caused that reaction?

He paused and glanced around, looking for a sign that anyone was nearby or anything was out of place.

He saw nothing.

The door was shut. The room was dark. Everything appeared as they'd left it.

But still, something seemed off.

"Kai?" Gage narrowed his eyes. "What's going on?"

"Just a gut feeling," he muttered.

Had someone been in this room while they were gone?

Kai didn't like the thought of that.

No one should have been able to follow them here. So who? And how?

Maybe he was overreacting. But he'd learned to trust his instincts.

His thoughts raced.

"Stay back," Kai told Tori and Stephen. "Gage, be ready to get them out of here if needed."

Then he drew his gun.

He opened the motel room door and quietly stepped inside.

When he hit the lights, he confirmed his instincts were right.

A man sat in a corner chair by the desk, facing him.

Waiting with no fear.

Waiting to make a statement.

———

Tori froze, wondering what Kai saw that caused him to tense so quickly.

Then she heard him mutter, "Larchmont?"

Her heart beat harder. Larchmont? Why had he come?

And he was in their motel room right now.

Gage pushed past her and peered inside before shaking his head. "What . . . ?"

"Come on inside." Kai motioned to her and Stephen with the sweep of his hand. "It's safe . . . relatively speaking, at least."

They flooded inside, Stephen still holding the towel over his shoulder. The bleeding appeared to have stopped, but he still needed medical help. Tori worried about the amount of blood he'd lost.

Kai locked the door behind them—after first glancing around one more time to make sure they hadn't been followed.

Tori stood near the door, watching as the three men walked closer to Larchmont, who sat at the corner table, looking as if he belonged there. The man was tall with a shock of white hair and distinguished features. His skin was tan, and he was probably in his late sixties, if she had to guess.

An air of authority surrounded him as he nodded at everyone before looking at her. "Hello, Tori."

Her lungs froze. "How do you know my name?"

"I know a lot of things."

Her gaze went to Kai and Gage, whose expressions were stony.

Then she glanced at Stephen. He showed no sign of recognition.

"How did you find us?" Kai demanded, a defensive edge to his voice and his hands firmly grounded on his hips.

"I was able to track you down after you called your colleagues to warn them about their implants."

"Our phones are encrypted," Gage said.

"I have my ways." Larchmont shrugged as if it

weren't a big deal. "Everything has a backup plan. *Everything.*"

Tori's mind still reeled as she stepped farther into the room.

Was it a good thing that Larchmont was here?

Or had he come to finish everyone off? She wasn't sure if she could trust him or not.

It appeared she was about to find out.

But while Kai and Gage asked him questions, she needed to continue to treat Stephen. There was no time to waste.

FORTY-THREE

KAI DIDN'T DARE SIT. He didn't want Larchmont to think he'd let down his guard.

Instead, he glared at his boss. "We need an explanation."

"We demand one." Gage cocked his head as he moved to stand on the other side of Larchmont.

Stephen sat on the edge of the bed, his skin pale. Kai heard Tori rifling through the first-aid kit, trying to find something to put on his wound.

But Kai's focus otherwise remained on Larchmont.

"I know you have a lot of questions," Larchmont started. "Maybe I can give you some answers. But you might want to sit down first."

"I'd rather stand," Kai said.

Gage offered a curt nod. "Me too."

"Very well then." Larchmont let out a breath before nodding. "What do you want to know?"

"More about Project Elevate, for starters," Kai said.

He let out another breath. "I suppose I should start at the beginning. Project Elevate was launched nearly twenty-five years ago as a joint effort between all the military branches. The Joint Chiefs of Staff sanctioned it."

Kai blinked when he heard the number. "Did you say it was started twenty-five years ago?"

"That's right," Larchmont said. "I wasn't there at the program's inception. In fact, for the first decade, the concept was in developmental stages. There were no test subjects."

Gage bristled. "I'm assuming we were considered test subjects?"

Larchmont nodded grimly, an almost apologetic look in his eyes. "That's correct. Stephen was in the first generation of our experiments, and he operated under a man known only as Rafferty."

"I don't remember you," Stephen said.

"I was more of a liaison for the program," he said. "I didn't work directly with you or the other guys you went through with. I took over after Rafferty was fired."

"Who exactly is Rafferty?" Stephen asked as Tori dabbed his wound with what looked like an antiseptic wipe. "I keep trying to find out more information on him, but he's like a ghost. He calls all the shots, but no one has ever seen his face. It's weird."

"Even though I officially worked with him, I don't know much about him," Larchmont said. "He was the man behind the curtain, so to speak. I only know he left the program under not-so-good circumstances. Many people weren't happy with him or his ethics."

"And the men under him?" Kai asked.

"They were let go. Many of the experiments done on them weren't considered a success."

Kai glanced at Stephen, trying to see his reaction. His expression remained calm as Tori continued to clean his wound.

"So Gage and I were in the second generation?" Kai continued, his mind still racing.

"That's right. That's when I took over. Before that, I was second in command, and I didn't like a lot of the things I saw. I was determined to make some changes and to not make the same mistakes made the first time."

"What kind of mistakes were those exactly?" Stephen narrowed his eyes, his voice strained and veins bulging at his neck.

Larchmont let out a long breath. "The experiments were too harsh and damaging. There was some work with electrical pulses and brainwaves.

Those experiments nearly wiped out some of the men's consciousnesses. We feared it had altered people's brain chemistry. Maybe even permanently. These men were also pushed to the limits. And in the end, they were . . . broken."

Kai fisted his hands at the thought. People shouldn't be disposable like that. Someone needed accountability for what they'd done.

Gage shifted. "And the pacemakers?"

"I heard Rafferty discussing it as an exit strategy in case things went wrong. He said we couldn't have people going rogue and causing collateral damage. It seemed a more humane option than shooting them dead."

"But you continued using that method with the second generation of soldiers," Kai said. "So you must have agreed."

Larchmont's expression remained stoic. "We did. The devices served various purposes, really. We could monitor heart rate. If it got too high or low, we could make corrections. It all tied in with the idea of being a super soldier. Then we could use the device for other purposes if our project went off the rails."

"Who controls these pacemakers?" Kai continued trying to put together the pieces.

"I did . . . for a while. Then we destroyed the remotes. However, we believe Rafferty was recently able to gain control of all the devices. He hacked into the system."

"You guys couldn't reprogram anything?" Gage asked. "Bypass some system controls or something?"

Larchmont ran a hand over his face, suddenly appearing exhausted. "We could not. We feared that Rafferty somehow blocked our efforts. He is that smart."

Based on his tone, Larchmont sounded like he was telling the truth. Yet Kai still couldn't be sure.

Kai tightened his arms across his chest, still in interrogation mode. "Why didn't you tell us?"

"Because I've been sworn to secrecy," Larchmont said. "It's a matter of national security."

"And these other guys?" Kai's voice rose. "The ones who made it through the program but weren't successful? What happened to them?"

"They're the ones who've been after you," Larchmont said.

"How do we stop them?" Gage asked.

His expression turned grim. "We can't. They've been programmed to be the way they are. The only way to stop them is by killing them."

"How about me? I'm innocent," Stephen said as Tori placed a bandage over his wound. "Am I on your list of people to kill?"

"No, you're not like the rest." Larchmont tilted

his head. "Why *are* you different from the rest of them? I've been curious about that for a while."

"I don't know," Stephen said. "I saw some of my colleagues go off the deep end and become . . . dark, for lack of a better word. A couple of us—including Nathan—weren't affected like that. We began working for Rafferty doing private missions."

"Can you confirm Rafferty is using these other men as his own personal soldiers for covert black-op missions?" Kai asked.

Stephen offered a curt nod. "Rafferty has them doing jobs he knows the rest of us won't do—ones that require abandoning any sense of morality or goodness."

His answer hung heavy in the air.

Kai wasn't surprised. But he knew the implications of Stephen's words.

He knew they were all in grave danger.

———

Tori listened to the conversation with interest. But she had a more pressing thought that she couldn't believe hadn't been brought up yet, something more important than the history of this program.

"We need to get these pacemaker-like devices out of these guys." Her voice came out strong and sure. "Now."

Surprise flickered through Larchmont's gaze before it settled with a nod. "I agree. But there will be challenges to doing that. For starters, taking you guys to a hospital is too risky—especially right now. You could be recognized. Also, there would be too many questions about the devices. It would raise some red flags. We can't risk that. The best way to tackle this is by doing so privately."

"What about the surgeons who implanted them?" Tori asked.

"We can't trust them."

Her mind raced. She glanced at Kai, who now stood near the window, peering out on occasion. That was Kai for you—always on guard.

She found a lot of comfort in the fact he was always so alert and responsible.

So protective—even if he was only that way because that was how he'd been trained.

"How have you even been changing the batteries?" Tori asked. "These guys have to be under sedation for the procedure."

Larchmont nodded slowly. "A lot of the experiments we did required sedation. The protocol wasn't ever questioned. When we took the guys in to do any type of procedure on them, we changed the batteries while they were sedated. Then we kept them sedated until they could heal."

Tori narrowed her eyes. "It seems like an over-reach if you ask me."

"Yes, I suppose it has been."

"How did my brother even get through this program?" Tori continued. "He was always kind with a good heart. He didn't change into one of the bad guys."

"Not everyone who went through the first generation turned out bad. Like your brother. Like Stephen. My understanding is that the recruiters who handpicked Nathan didn't know at the time that you were trying to reconnect with him. That became a problem since we prefer the men who go through the program to be unattached."

"I find it despicable." Tori didn't hold back how she felt. "How can you even sleep at night? How can you live with yourself, for that matter?"

Larchmont's gaze darkened. "I've only tried to protect my men."

"The same men you've used and lied to, you mean?" Tori's tone remained biting.

Silence stretched a minute.

Larchmont apparently didn't know how to respond to that.

Kai paused near a window and frowned. "You guys, there's movement outside. I'm nearly certain the police have us surrounded."

FORTY-FOUR

A SENSE of urgency raced through Kai. "If the police surround this place, there's no way we're getting out. Not without taking some of them down, and I'm not willing to do that. These cops are just doing their jobs also. I don't want to see anyone else hurt."

Larchmont stood. "I was afraid this might happen. We need to head to the roof."

Kai stiffened. "The roof?"

"Just trust me."

His mind raced. The last thing he wanted to do was to trust Larchmont. But it didn't appear as if they had any choice.

"If we're going to get up there, then we need to move." Larchmont snapped back into leader mode. "Now."

Kai wanted to argue with Larchmont's words, but he couldn't. It was either they acted now, or they turned themselves in. He wasn't ready to turn himself in yet.

He and Gage exchanged a glance. Gage nodded, confirming they should listen to Larchmont.

They didn't have any other options right now, and Kai knew the last thing Larchmont wanted was for them to be arrested. Too many details about their past might come out if they were.

Kai turned to Stephen. "Are you okay to move?"

"I did a quick cleanup of his wound," Tori said. "He'll need more medical attention, but for now I put a bandage on him."

"Okay then." Kai nodded toward the door. "Grab anything you need, and let's get moving."

Kai opened the door in time to see the flashing lights outside.

How did they even get onto the roof from here?

"To the left," Larchmont said as if he'd already thought this out. He took the lead and led them down the walkway past several rooms and then took another left into an alcove.

He stopped when he came to a ladder.

Kai pulled down the guard over it, and the ladder crashed down.

"Police!" an officer called from a bullhorn below. "Stop what you're doing!"

Kai glanced back. At least four cars had pulled into the parking lot.

This didn't look good.

He motioned for Tori to go first. She trembled in front of him as she climbed the ladder.

He scrambled up behind her, and the rest of the gang followed.

When they got to the roof, Kai's heart pounded in his ears. There was nothing except for some HVAC equipment up here. No place to hide. Nowhere to go.

What exactly had Larchmont's plan been? Had this been a trap?

Kai sent his boss a questioning look.

"You'll see," Larchmont assured them.

"Come down from the roof!" an officer called through a bullhorn from below.

Kai had seen the police in the parking lot. Each of the officers was posed for action behind their police cars, doors opened and guns drawn.

These men thought they were tracking killers.

Kai couldn't even blame them for that.

It appeared Kai, Gage, and Tori were in even more hot water.

Then he heard a chopping sound from above.

He glanced up at the dark sky.

The sound grew louder as a light appeared, swooping toward them.

A helicopter, Kai realized. Larchmont had arranged for a helicopter to come pick them up.

———

As Tori climbed into her seat, her head whirled along with the blades above her.

A helicopter?

Larchmont really *had* thought this through.

But they still weren't out of danger.

What if the cops shot down the helicopter? Did they have the capability of doing that?

Even if these officers didn't have the capability, certainly they could bring in someone who could bring the aircraft down.

Unless this copter got out of here fast.

But still, air traffic control would track them somehow.

Tori couldn't think about those details right now. They just needed to concentrate on getting out of here.

As soon as everyone was inside and the doors were closed, the pilot lifted into the air. Tori tried to jerk her seatbelt in place, but her hands were shaking too badly.

Kai reached over her and pulled the belt over her lap, snapping it in place.

She let out a breath and murmured, "Thanks."

The aircraft rocked as it climbed higher.

Tori pressed her eyes closed, trying to keep her fear under control. Doing so took all her energy.

"They're still going to track us!" Kai yelled over the noise of the copter.

"Yes, but we just bought some time," Larchmont yelled back from the front. "Now that Rafferty knows you know, he's going to want to take you down."

"Where are we going?" Gage asked above the roar of the copter.

Larchmont called over his shoulder, "I have a safe house secured. We'll be okay there for a while."

Tori's thoughts continued to race.

She wanted to trust that these people knew what they were doing. That Larchmont was in their corner.

But she wasn't ready to concede that.

They climbed into the night sky, leaving the motel and the flashing police cars beneath them.

She continued to monitor Stephen as they flew. He was holding steady for the time being.

They headed away from the city, and the lights faded from plentiful to scattered.

Tori couldn't be sure, but it almost looked like mountains were below them.

Being in a helicopter at night surrounded by mountains? Not ideal.

Kai seemed to sense her anxiety. He reached over and squeezed her hand.

Tori offered him a soft smile.

Maybe he even understood the apprehension also.

Thirty minutes after they'd taken off, the helicopter shifted as it prepared to land.

But when they landed, she wasn't sure what—or who—they would face.

It might be someone who could help them.

Or it could be another enemy.

CHAPTER
FORTY-FIVE

KAI DIDN'T LIKE any of this. He still wasn't sure if he could trust Larchmont. And trusting the wrong person could get them all killed.

But they had little choice right now.

They landed in an open field in the middle of what appeared to be nowhere. An SUV waited there, Trevor behind the wheel.

They disembarked from the copter and headed toward the waiting vehicle. Wasting no time, they all piled in. Larchmont climbed into the front seat. He tapped the dashboard, indicating to Trevor that he should get moving.

As they sped from the area, the helicopter became airborne again. It was the quickest exchange he'd ever seen. But Kai knew it was better that way.

Gage turned toward Larchmont. "How did you have all that planned?"

"I always have an exit plan," Larchmont stated as he looked ahead. "Always. I thought I taught you guys that also."

"You did," Kai said. "But all of this . . ."

"A simple thank you would be sufficient."

Kai's jaw hardened. There were definitely things he'd like to say to the man other than thank you. But for now, he kept his mouth shut.

Instead, he glanced around him at the dark, rolling landscape. It was hard to see very much, but his instincts told him they'd landed in the Georgia mountains. This area was probably an ideal place to hide out since the population was low.

As they drove, Kai grabbed Tori's hand again. He told himself he did so to comfort her. But her touch did just as much to comfort him, even if he didn't want to admit it.

She was scared, and rightly so. Kai also had so many uncertainties. He hoped they weren't headed from one trap into another.

Thirty minutes later, they pulled up to an isolated log cabin nestled on the side of a hill and surrounded by trees. No neighbors were in sight.

At first glance, the place seemed safe enough.

Kai prayed they'd be secure here tonight.

They needed to get somewhere where they could continue to treat Stephen's injuries. He knew Tori had begun to clean him up, but there was still more to be done.

Also, there were still more answers they needed to find out.

Time was running out, and more than one life was on the line.

———

Once at the cabin, Tori had done her best to treat Stephen's wound.

Larchmont had some medical supplies waiting for them, including some pain pills. Those had helped Stephen get through the next excruciating moments.

She'd had to remove a couple of broken pieces of the tracker from inside him. She knew that it didn't feel good. But she had no other choice. She couldn't leave the parts in there to cause infection.

Stephen was resting now in one of the spare bedrooms. His body needed to heal, and sleep was one of the best ways to do this. Plus, he'd spiked a fever, which had her concerned. She'd need to keep an eye on that.

Tori knew the rest of the guys would need some

time to talk among themselves. Her head was already about to explode from everything she'd already heard and was trying to process. She didn't need to learn anything else.

Instead, she went into a private bathroom inside one of the bedrooms and began to scrub her hands. She'd used gloves when she worked on Stephen, but she still felt the need to clean herself up.

How her life had changed over the past couple of weeks was unbelievable. The simple days of going into work at different hospitals were now long gone.

Would her life ever be the same? She wasn't sure.

Just as Tori came out of the bathroom, someone knocked at the bedroom door. "Tori, it's me. Kai. Can I come in?"

Her heart rate quickened when she heard Kai's voice. She walked to the door and opened it.

Her heart stammered even faster when she saw him standing there. When she remembered the feel of his hand in hers.

Was it possible that she'd finally met the man of her dreams . . . while in the middle of running for her life?

Not ideal. She wasn't even sure her emotions in this situation could be trusted.

Yet the other part of her so desperately wanted to dive into those very emotions.

Kai Kaleo was unlike anyone she'd ever met before. All she wanted was to get to know him more.

That also seemed like such a bad idea.

"Can we talk a minute?" He kept his voice low as he asked the question.

"Of course." She let him into the bedroom.

He closed the door behind him, and they both sat on the edge of the bed. Only the soft glow of a lamp on the nightstand lit the room.

"Are you doing okay?" he started, his voice earnest and concerned as he peered at her, the dim light softening his normally hard features.

How was she doing? How did she answer that honestly?

Finally, she said, "This is a lot."

"Yes, it is."

Tori studied his face as she wondered about the sudden change in him from earlier. Too much was at stake right now for her to beat around the bush. "You're not avoiding me anymore?"

She was seriously curious about the change in him. After their talk last night, he'd definitely put up a wall. Tori hadn't been sure that wall would ever come down. The barrier had seemed high and impenetrable.

So what had changed?

"Tori . . ." His voice turned hoarse as his gaze

flickered up to meet hers. "You shouldn't get involved with someone like me. I'd be doing an injustice to you if I let you believe otherwise."

"What do you mean someone like you?"

"Danger follows me everywhere."

"Isn't it up to me to determine if I want to take that chance?" She stared at him, trying desperately to see the truth in his eyes.

As their gazes connected, she finally understood.

Kai was beginning to care about her just as much as Tori was beginning to care about him. Yet he was trying to look out for her, to keep her safe.

Really, it was sweet.

But that shouldn't just be his decision either.

"Kai . . ." She reached up and gently ran her thumb against his cheek, feeling the start of unshaven stubble. His scent, part Ivory soap and part evergreen cologne, rose up to her. She hadn't even realized how familiar the smell had become—or how much she enjoyed it.

He reached for her waist and pulled her closer.

Tori's throat went dry as she anticipated what might happen next. As she imagined what it might be like to feel his lips against hers.

Speaking of lips . . . her gaze went to his mouth. Then back to his eyes. Then to his mouth again.

Kai leaned closer, and she closed her eyes.

Before their lips touched, a commotion sounded in the hallway.

"Kai! Tori! We need you."

They sprang away from each other and toward the door.

What had happened now?

FORTY-SIX

KAI DARTED into the kitchen and froze.

Stephen lay on the floor, pale and unmoving.

Gage knelt beside him, his finger to the man's neck. "He doesn't have a pulse!"

Kai sucked in a breath. He knew exactly what that meant.

His worst fears were confirmed.

Someone—Rafferty, most likely—had used that pacemaker to his advantage.

Tori rushed past Kai to Stephen. She began CPR. "I need a defibrillator. Do we have one?"

"I brought one," Larchmont said. "I'll get it."

He reappeared a moment later with the device.

Working quickly, Tori tore off Stephen's shirt. Then she charged the machine and put the electrical nodules on Stephen's chest.

"Clear!" she called out, indicating for everyone to stay back.

Kai held his breath as Tori hit the button to activate the machine.

The machine buzzed before an electrical pulse went through Stephen.

Kai kept his eyes on Stephen as he prayed.

But there was nothing.

Tori activated the machine again.

This time, Stephen's eyes jerked open, and he sucked in a long, almost painful-sounding breath.

Kai exhaled. He was alive. Tori had brought him back.

But if the person controlling that pacemaker learned of that, they might activate it again. At any minute.

Tori still knelt beside Stephen. But she raised her gaze to meet Kai's.

He saw the worry in her eyes—worry that the same thing that happened to Stephen would also happen to Kai.

It was a definite possibility, one none of them could deny.

He glanced at Larchmont, who stood with them, a worried expression on his face.

"How do we find this Rafferty guy?" Kai's voice sounded hard and determined—reflecting everything he felt inside.

From what he understood so far, Rafferty might be the only one with answers.

Larchmont's expression remained tight. "That's going to be difficult."

"Why is that?" Kai asked.

"Because he's a . . . ghost."

———

Kai couldn't take this anymore. All the secrets. He wasn't sure what Larchmont knew and what the man simply wasn't sharing with them.

And Kai didn't like being in the dark.

"Can I have a moment?" he asked Larchmont.

His boss followed him down the hallway where they'd have some privacy.

"What do you know about Rafferty?" Kai started. "Because if he's the one controlling these pacemakers then we need to find him."

"Like I said earlier, he's a mystery. He's a brilliant scientist—and a little too determined. He was angry when he was fired. Took it personally. Then he disappeared and took his men with him. The government considered him a threat, but they were never able to locate him."

"So they just let him go with these super soldiers?" Kai didn't bother to hide the disgust from his voice. How irresponsible was that?

"They were concerned, to be sure," Larchmont said. "I think they secretly hoped these guys would just all go away and never be seen again. Besides, it's not like the government could own up to what they'd done. Can you imagine the lawsuits? Instead, they sent men to kill everyone involved. However, all the men they sent out to erase the soldiers under Rafferty ended up dead."

Kai shook his head. He could believe a lot of things. He'd seen a lot of things.

But this even surprised him.

How had someone gotten away with this?

"This guy is going to kill us all." Kai's words hung in the air.

Larchmont maintained his perfectly controlled façade. "I can get you a surgeon, but you'll need a hospital."

"If we go to the hospital then we'll be arrested," Kai said.

"Correct."

Kai raked a hand through his hair and then shook his head. "I can't believe you didn't tell us this."

"My hands were tied. I had to make some hard decisions."

"And now we're all at risk." Accusation stained Kai's voice.

"I know—and I'm sorry."

However, sorry didn't seem like enough, all things considered.

TORI SAT beside Stephen's bed, monitoring his progress as the night drew on. Since he'd developed a fever an hour ago, she feared infection was kicking in from his bullet wound.

She didn't dare leave him alone, fearful that something else might happen to him.

But she supposed the same could be said for any of these guys.

Her heart thudded with apprehension at the thought.

What if something happened to all of them at once? How could she help them all? And the defibrillator . . . they only had one. How could she possibly pick who to treat?

She tried to push down her worries and anxiety as she thought of her favorite Scriptures.

Philippians 4:6–7: Do not be anxious about anything, but in everything by prayer and supplication with thanksgiving let your requests be made known to God. And the peace of God, which surpasses all understanding, will guard your hearts and your minds in Christ Jesus.

Joshua 1:9: Have I not commanded you? Be strong and courageous. Do not be frightened, and do not be dismayed, for the Lord your God is with you wherever you go.

Matthew 6:34: Therefore do not be anxious about tomorrow, for tomorrow will be anxious for itself. Sufficient for the day is its own trouble.

Still, the reality of the situation continued to hit her. This whole thing felt impossible.

Would Larchmont really be able to set up surgery? Or could they find the person who controlled the pacemakers and stop him?

She had no idea if either of those things were possible.

Or if they could even track down this Rafferty guy . . . maybe he would have some answers.

Each of those things were out of her control. All she could do was take care of anyone who was injured—which was an important job.

She only wished there was a way she could help prevent all of this. But that wasn't within her power. She rubbed a hand over her face, feeling the tension in her brow and jaws.

Someone poked his head around the corner. As Kai's face came into view, Tori's shoulders softened.

Somehow, seeing him always made her feel better.

He paced closer and glanced at Stephen, who still slept. "How's it going?"

"He's stable. I'm just glad I was close when this happened and that we had the right equipment we needed."

"Me too," he said solemnly. "I'm here to relieve you. I can sit with him for a while so you can get some rest."

"But you need your rest also."

"I already got some. I insist that you go. I'll get you if I need you. I promise."

Tori glanced at Stephen one more moment before nodding and standing. She was tired. In fact, her whole body had begun to ache, beginning to bear the strain of this situation.

"Okay then," she finally conceded. "As long as you promise to get me."

"I do."

She started to walk past him when he touched her arm. When she looked up at him, their gazes caught.

He pulled her to him and wrapped her in his arms.

There wasn't anything romantic about the motion. He was simply offering comfort.

And it worked.

Her body softened in his embrace.

It had been a long time since she'd had this kind of human contact. Probably since Michael—and he'd been a mistake, the picture of steadfastness on the outside. But it was all an act.

Their breakup had only solidified her need to keep her distance from people.

As a traveling nurse, so many of her relationships —friendships—were short-term. Then, just as she got close to people, it was time for her to move on to a new location.

Her hesitancy to get too close to people was partly borne from her past in foster care. It was always safer to keep your distance, to not depend on anyone.

So why did Tori feel like she wanted to do this with Kai always and forever?

It was a dangerous thought—especially since Kai had made it clear he wasn't looking for a relationship.

When this was over, he would most likely move on. So would she.

She'd be wise to keep that in mind.

———

Kai sat beside Stephen.

Right now, everyone had their own jobs to do.

Gage was keeping an eye on the outside of the house in case anyone caught wind that they were staying here. Trevor was trying to find the actual security footage from Landon Jean-Pierre's house by hacking into the server of the security company. Someone had clearly altered the one sent to the police. Larchmont was trying to find a medical facility for their surgeries.

As Kai sat there, his mind drifted. He remembered the feeling of having Tori in his arms.

As soon as they'd stepped apart from each other, he missed her.

That thought was crazy.

But as much as he tried to deny those feelings, he knew they were there. If he were smart, he wouldn't deny them. He would deal with them and move on.

Yet he couldn't get the woman out of his head, even though he had far more urgent things to think about right now.

She'd disappeared into her bedroom.

Kai absently rubbed his chest again. He kept catching himself doing that. He was all too aware that he could be in Stephen's situation at any point.

He was living on borrowed time, and he didn't like that thought.

"Kai . . ." Stephen murmured.

He jerked his head toward the man and saw that his eyes had fluttered open.

"Are you okay?" Kai stood and leaned closer. "Do I need to get Tori?"

Stephen shook his head, his skin pale and his eyes dull.

"I remembered . . . something," the man said, his voice hoarse.

"About what?"

"Rafferty . . ."

Stephen had all his attention right now. "What did you remember?"

"Overheard one of his minions . . . said he likes to stay close," Stephen rasped. "Something about a bunker."

A bunker? Kai mused. That was interesting. But did that information really help them? He wasn't sure.

His mind raced as he tried to figure out what to do with that. Without more information, what Stephen had told him was just that—information.

But he prayed he'd find more pieces to this puzzle soon.

FORTY-EIGHT

JUST AS THE sun began to rise the next morning, Kai's phone buzzed.

The phone was encrypted, and even though Larchmont had been able to track them through it, no one else should be able to. Kai wanted to keep in touch with the rest of his colleagues just in case something happened to them as well.

He prayed that wasn't the case, but he couldn't stop thinking about the possibility.

He'd been sitting with Stephen all night, and the man had been fast asleep. His fever was holding steady and not rising—something for which Kai was extremely grateful.

He glanced at his screen and saw that it was a text from . . . Alfie?

> I might have some info on Landon.

The man definitely had Kai's attention now.
Kai texted back:

> What kind of information?

> They cleaned out his locker at the golf club. I happened to be nearby when they did. He had a cell phone stashed there, and I grabbed it before anyone saw me. This wasn't his everyday cell phone. I wonder if there's something on it that could help you figure out what happened to him. I can't stop thinking about how he was murdered. Whoever did it needs to be brought to justice.

Kai let that sink in for a minute. That cell phone could prove to be valuable.

But he still had some reservations.

Kai texted:

> Why did you decide to tell me this?

> I've seen your picture on the news. But my gut tells me you're not behind what happened to Landon. I want to know who did this. I'm no investigator, but I have a feeling you are. I hope you can figure something out.

Kai stared at the words a moment before texting back a thank-you.

He needed to find Gage and let him know about this update. Then they could decide whether or not they wanted to share this information with Larchmont.

———

Tori awoke after a restless night. She'd tried to sleep. When she couldn't, she'd found herself researching pacemakers and what was involved in either removing them or deactivating them.

Though she was armed with more knowledge now, she knew there was still very little she could do given the limitations here at the cabin and her lack of experience.

After getting dressed, she wandered into the kitchen to get some coffee just in time to overhear Kai and Gage talking. She didn't intend to eavesdrop, but she'd walked into the middle of it without realizing it.

They were talking about meeting Alfie, who apparently had some new information for them. That seemed like a terrible idea, all things considered.

"You two are leaving?" Panic tried to seize her at that thought.

The two of them were safer staying here out of

sight, especially until Larchmont was closer to finding a surgery center that could remove their pacemakers. Didn't they know that? Especially after what had happened to Stephen yesterday?

Kai turned to her, a mug of coffee in his hand as he lingered near the pot. "This might be the only way that we can find answers."

"There has to be something else you can do." Her voice held an almost pleading sound. "Someone else that you can send."

"Unfortunately, we're the ones who know the most about this. We make the most sense."

Tori wanted to argue, but she couldn't. His words were true.

Instead, she propped her hip against the kitchen counter, afraid she might lose her balance. The thought of Kai leaving made her feel lightheaded.

"Larchmont is closer to finding a place to do our surgery," he told her. "We're going to get to the bottom of this."

"I hope so." She drew in a shaky breath, trying to hold herself together. "How's Stephen?"

"He's stable. Trevor is with him. But we're going to need you to stay with him."

"Who's going to meet Alfie?" She held her breath as she waited for his response.

"Just Gage and I. The fewer of us out there, the better."

Kai was right. Tori's best bet was to stay here and to keep an eye on Stephen to make sure he was okay.

Still, she worried about those two being out there—especially with the police and these other guys looking for them.

She knew that arguing with Kai would do no good. So she nodded.

Then she took it to the next level and began to pray.

KAI AND GAGE left to get the cell phone, hoping this risk was worth it.

As they drove through the mountains, Kai kept his eyes wide open. They were a good thirty minutes away from where they were meeting Alfie.

The rest of the team was still trying to figure out who Rafferty really was and any other information they could find out about him. Larchmont had called in some favors, but he didn't sound hopeful. Larchmont was also working to secure a location to have their pacemakers removed. Trevor said he was close to getting the actual security footage from Landon Jean-Pierre's house.

Maybe they would make some progress.

Finally, Kai and Gage pulled over at the rest stop where they were supposed to meet Alfie.

The area was public enough—but public could be a good or bad thing.

Kai and Gage could be recognized as wanted killers.

But it also meant that if this was a setup, other people would be around.

Which meant those very people could be hurt.

Kai pressed his lips together. There was no good way to do this.

He glanced at Gage. "You ready for this?"

"I'm ready to find some answers."

"Then let's go."

They climbed from the SUV in time to see Alfie pull into a parking space not far away.

This was it.

Kai prayed the meeting went well.

———

Tori found herself distracted as she thought about what Kai and Gage might be doing right now.

She couldn't stop praying for their well-being.

Part of her wished she was there with them, though she knew her presence would do no good.

Still, she hated not knowing what was going on.

As Stephen began to stir beside her, Tori took his temperature again.

It still held steady. Though that was a good thing,

she prayed he might get some real medical help soon. If he took a turn for the worse, there would be little she could do.

"Where are the rest of the guys?" Stephen blinked, every action appearing as if it took painful effort.

Tori turned toward him. "They went to meet a guy named Alfie."

He squinted. "Who is Alfie?"

"He was a friend of Dr. Jean-Pierre, the man we're accused of killing." She pulled out her phone, found the picture she'd taken of him outside the apartment building, and showed it to Stephen.

His eyes widened. "His name isn't Alfie."

Tori's muscles snapped taut. "What do you mean?"

He raised a hand and pointed his finger at her screen. "His name is Rocky. He and I went through Project Elevate together."

Her heart nearly stopped. Certainly, she hadn't heard Stephen correctly. "What?"

Stephen's gaze suddenly looked much more alert. "He became Rafferty's right-hand man."

"Are you sure?"

"Positive."

Tori stood, panic racing through her. "I have to let Kai and Gage know. They've been set up."

She quickly dialed Kai's number.

But there was no answer.

More panic bombarded her.

She dialed again, desperate to get through.

But again, no answer.

How was she going to warn them?

Tori had to somehow figure out a way to stop them before they got themselves killed.

KAI NODDED AT ALFIE. Though the man appeared to be helpful, Kai needed to be careful not to trust anyone too much. Not given these circumstances.

If Alfie was telling the truth, then this cell phone he'd obtained could be pivotal to finding answers. But the mere fact that Alfie trusted them so easily and wanted to help also raised red flags.

He and Gage would need to be on guard.

"Thanks for coming." Alfie paused in front of them, wearing khakis and a button-up shirt. He looked as if he'd just come from another day of peddling meds at doctor's offices across Atlanta. "I wasn't sure if you'd show up."

"We weren't sure you'd show up either." Kai's muscles remained stiff. "But we appreciate you coming to us with this information you discovered. It was risky for you to take Landon's phone."

"I know." Alfie shrugged. "But it seemed as if it might be worth it."

"This could be the smoking gun we're looking for," Gage said. "Do you have it with you?"

Alfie reached into his pocket and handed over a basic black cell phone. "Hopefully, you guys can get it unlocked. Doing that is above my skill level."

"We have people who can help us," Kai said. "I hope we can find something on it. Have you tried to unlock it?"

A frown twisted Alfie's lips. "I have to admit I *did* try one code just for fun. I used Landon's best golfing score—he bragged about it all the time. 0069. I thought it might be worth a shot, but I had no luck."

"Thanks again." Kai raised the phone and took a step back. He didn't want to waste any more time, especially considering the severity of the situation. "We need to run."

"What are you going to do now?" Alfie remained in the parking lot as if he wanted more information.

"We'll do our best to unlock this," Kai told him. "We'll see what kind of information we might be able to find on it. Maybe text messages or phone numbers or even internet searches. It's hard to say. But maybe something on it will lead us to the person who killed Landon."

"That's all I want." Alfie's face tightened with determination. "I just want justice for my friend. Will you let me know what happens?"

"We'll do our best," Gage said. "But it might take a while. Our first priority is finding whoever did this. We also need to keep our heads down so the police don't find us. Because if they find us before we know who's guilty, then we're going to end up behind bars."

Alfie's gaze remained serious. "I hope that doesn't happen."

"So do we." Kai took another step back. "Now we need to see what we can do to find those answers. But thank you again. If you could not tell anyone that you saw us . . . that would be fantastic."

"Of course," he said. "Best of luck."

Kai and Gage walked back to the SUV. Kai watched Alfie climb back into his car and drive away before turning back to the cell phone.

Gage plugged in a device that helped them to determine what codes were used to unlock phones. In situations like this, using technology was much easier than trying to take random guesses, only to end up totally locked out.

But it would also take some time—and time was something that they didn't have.

As they waited, Kai glanced at his phone. No updates.

Then he squinted. He didn't have a signal.

Strange. Rest stops usually had service.

Kai glanced at Gage. "Do you have any bars on your phone?"

Gage glanced at his own screen and shook his head. "No, I don't."

Kai didn't like that realization. Didn't like the thought that other people might not be able to get in touch with him right now if they needed to.

But soon enough, he hoped they would have some answers.

Knowing the truth might give them all a little more peace of mind.

Tori called Kai's number one more time, but nothing happened.

Anxiety stirred inside her.

Something was wrong. She was certain of it.

She raced through the house looking for Larchmont. She found him sitting at the dining room table with a computer in front of him.

"I keep trying to get through to Kai and Gage," she started, her words coming out too fast. "I think they're being set up. Stephen recognized Alfie's picture. Said his name wasn't Alfie but some guy named Rocky."

Larchmont's eyes widened. "Rocky Velasquez?"

"He didn't say a last name."

"Let me see the picture."

She found it on her phone and showed it to him.

His face went paler. "That's one of Rafferty's guys. This whole time he was pretending to be someone he wasn't. I wish I'd seen this earlier . . ."

Her pulse surged. "I'm trying to warn Kai, but no one is answering."

"Rocky is probably using some type of jammer on their numbers."

"So how can we help them?"

Larchmont stood. "Trevor and I will track them down at the rest area."

"I want to go too. They may need my help."

"I need you to stay with Stephen."

"I'll be fine." A deep voice cut into their conversation.

Tori looked up and saw that Stephen had followed her into the dining room.

He looked pale and his eyes dull, but he still looked so much better than he had earlier.

She prayed the worst was over for him.

But what had she been thinking? She couldn't leave him here.

It wasn't smart.

"I won't be any help out on the battlefield." He

leaned against the wall, still weak. "But I can hold my own for a little bit while you're gone."

She glanced at Larchmont who gave a brief nod.

"I have mixed feelings about you coming with us," Larchmont finally said. "But you're right. We might need you. Grab the first aid kit and the defibrillator, just in case."

Relief swept through her, followed by a wave of anxiety.

This could be terrifying.

But if Kai needed help, Tori wanted to be there. For Gage too.

She had pulled them into this mess. She would help them get out of it.

Even if it meant risking her life.

"IT'S UNLOCKED," Gage announced as he and Kai sat in the SUV. "Now let's see what's on this phone."

Kai leaned closer so he could also see. But he kept one eye open for anyone suspicious. At any moment, he halfway expected the police to surround them or for Rafferty's guys to show up.

But so far, everything was quiet.

"The doctor did get some texts," Gage murmured. "But I'm not really sure what to make of them. They don't scream that he was up to something."

"Most people don't have burner phones unless they're up to something," Kai pointed out.

"Good point. Let me check out his other messages."

Gage scrolled through and let out a grunt.

"What is it?" Kai asked.

"It looks like someone was manipulating him. Listen to this: Fake the test results. Landon responded: I can't lie to my friend. Then there's a picture of Tori with the words: Tell the truth and she'll die. Landon finally asked what the sender wanted him to do. The sender said, pretend everything is fine. We will kill her otherwise, so sell it."

"Wow. I guess that explains Landon's involvement."

"I'd say it does," Gage muttered.

"Look on maps," Kai said. "Let's see where he's been going lately."

Gage did that and looked into recent trips Landon had taken.

On three separate occasions, he went to a location in the middle of nowhere.

If Rafferty had forced Landon to lie about the results of Nathan's examination, there was a possibility that Rafferty was still trying to hold some type of leverage over him.

Maybe that was what had gotten Landon killed.

Kai's gut twisted at the thought of everything that had happened and the lengths these people had gone through to get what they wanted.

It was sickening.

"This place . . ." Gage murmured as he stared at

the map on his phone. "It's not actually that far from where we're staying."

"We should head there," Kai said.

"But if this place is what I think it is, we're going to need more than the two of us there."

Kai couldn't argue with that. He glanced at his phone again, but he still had no signal.

He couldn't even call his colleagues and give them an update. But maybe once they were on the road he could.

Landon's cell phone also didn't have any service.

"Let's head back to the cabin for that backup," Kai said. "Then we'll form a plan for finding this Rafferty guy. We'll play it safe and make sure all our bases are covered."

They headed down the road, back to the cabin that Larchmont had rented for them. As they got closer, Gage slowed.

A bad feeling brewed in Kai's gut—though he couldn't put his finger on why. Just finely tuned instincts.

"Gage . . . we shouldn't announce our arrival, just in case," Kai said.

"You think something's wrong?"

"I think it's a really good possibility."

Gage glanced at him another long moment before nodding. "Okay then. Let's play this safe."

Gage pulled off onto the side of the road. Then

they both climbed out and started toward the cabin. They gripped their guns as they approached.

But as Kai got closer, he realized that Larchmont's vehicle—he'd had one waiting here at the cabin—was no longer in the driveway.

He frowned.

Where had Larchmont gone? Had he taken Tori, Trevor, and Stephen with him?

Kai wasn't sure, but he needed to find out.

Tori continued to stare at her phone as she tried to reach Kai or Gage.

But it was no use.

Larchmont was probably correct. Some type of jammer had most likely been used.

That only meant trouble. Lots and lots of trouble for Kai and Gage.

She pressed her eyes closed. *Dear Lord, please be with them. Protect them. Help us help them.*

They headed down the road, toward the rest area.

But when they reached the meeting spot, there was no sign of Kai and Gage.

She glanced at her phone again. Before she could dial any numbers, Larchmont turned to her and held up his phone. A map filled the screen.

"What's that?"

"It's the tracking device I put on their SUV."

"You did what?" She didn't hide the incredulousness from her voice.

"It's just a precaution—perfect for times like these."

She didn't argue. Not right now.

Instead, she leaned closer. "Where are they?"

His jaw hardened. "It looks like they went back to the cabin."

She squinted in confusion. "I don't understand . . ."

"Most likely, Alfie wanted to meet them so he could follow them back to the house."

"What? Wouldn't we have passed them?"

"If we passed them while on the highway, we might not have even noticed them." Larchmont suddenly squealed out of the parking lot. "We need to warn them."

"Should we try to call again?"

"Let's try to text them, at least. But I'm not hopeful it will go through."

"What if we're too late?" She pulled up Kai's number, fingers poised to send him a text.

Larchmont's jaw hardened. "All we can do right now is get there as soon as we can and hope for the best."

KAI AND GAGE carefully approached the house.

As they got closer, they peered in the windows.

But they saw no one.

Still, they needed to remain on guard.

He nodded toward Gage, and Gage opened the front door.

He slipped inside, Kai following behind. They stayed near the walls as they walked through the cabin, looking for any signs of anything that was amiss.

But other than Tori, Larchmont, Trevor, and Stephen being gone, everything appeared to be in place.

Had something happened to Stephen? Had they rushed him to the hospital?

It could be a possibility.

Still, they crept past the living room and kitchen area.

Then they reached the hall leading to the bedrooms.

When he opened the first door, a shadowy figure appeared.

Kai swung his gun toward the man.

"Whoa." The man raised his hands. "It's just me. Stephen."

Kai let out his breath and lowered his weapon as Stephen came into focus. He was still pale, and his actions were weak, but at least he was walking around now. That was a big step.

"Where's everybody else?" he asked, shoving his gun into his waistband.

"Looking for you."

"Why did they go out looking for us?" Gage asked.

"Because your phones weren't working so they couldn't call and warn you."

"Warn us about what?" Kai wasn't sure what he was talking about.

"About Alfie—"

But before he could finish his statement, glass broke.

A loud bang filled the air, followed by smoke and bright flashes.

Kai coughed, his ears ringing.

A flashbang. Someone had thrown a flashbang inside to disorient them.

Kai squinted and raised his gun.

Someone was inside. Someone uninvited.

Someone who'd been waiting for the opportunity to ambush them.

He and Gage ducked into two bedrooms across the hall from each other and peered around the doorframes so they could have cover.

They watched as six men filtered into the house.

One of them came into view.

Kai sucked in a breath.

It was Alfie.

———

As far as Tori was concerned, she, Larchmont, and Trevor couldn't get back to the cabin fast enough. She had no idea what was going on there, but her gut told her it wasn't anything good.

She continued to pray, all while keeping her eyes open in case danger was close.

Near the cabin, something in the woods caught her eye.

She grabbed Larchmont's arm and pointed. "It's a car. Hidden in the brush."

Larchmont hit the brakes. "We're too late."

"Never say that," Tori said. "We don't know what's happening yet. We could still help."

"You're right," Larchmont said. "We can. We're just going to have to play it smart here, okay?"

She and Trevor nodded their agreement.

Larchmont pulled to the side of the road also and drew his gun. "Trevor, come with me. Tori, you wait here."

"What if they need me?" Tori touched the defibrillator in the seat beside her.

His gaze softened. Then he reached into his coat pocket and pressed something into her hand.

She stared at the cold, hard object in her grip.

A gun.

"Have you ever shot before?" Larchmont asked.

She nodded, suddenly feeling shaky. "I have."

"Then you know what to do?"

She nodded again, swallowing hard to push down her fear. "I do."

She didn't conceal carry, but as a single woman, she liked to stay up to date with her shooting skills . . . just in case.

"Now I have a gun, but what are we doing?"

"We need to get closer to see what's going on," Larchmont said. "But you let Trevor and I take the lead. Your main goal will be if anything happens you'll need to offer the medical help we need. Got it?"

She was comfortable with that agreement. "Got it."

They climbed out of the car and approached the cabin.

Tori continued to pray for safety . . . even as her life flashed before her eyes.

FIFTY-THREE

KAI WATCHED as Alfie stepped closer.

"Stay right there!" Kai shouted.

"I don't think you're in a position to call any shots."

"That's debatable," Kai said.

Alfie's gaze focused on something behind him, and he squinted. "You're alive, Stephen? I thought we'd finished you off?"

"You tried." Stephen touched his chest. "But you failed."

"It's not too late to finish what we started." Alfie's eyes glimmered.

"You were involved with this the whole time?" Kai asked. "You were a part of Landon's death, weren't you? In fact, you're probably the one who killed him and arranged that video so we would look as if we were guilty instead of you."

His smirk was all the answer they needed.

"Why?" Kai asked. "Why are you doing all of this?"

"Because people started asking too many questions. Got too many people involved. All Nathan and his friend had to do was leave this alone. But they couldn't do that. Then you guys had to get involved. You don't understand the extents we'll go through to keep our secrets quiet."

"You're just being used as a puppet."

Alfie scowled. "You have no idea."

"I'd say I do," Kai said. "Because we're in the same boat. You think you have the upper hand, but you don't. We're all being controlled."

"Stop talking!" Alfie sliced his hand through the air. "Rafferty has a plan, and we're just following orders. In the end, it will all be worth it."

"Why are you here?" Kai asked. "You could have stopped our hearts if you wanted to kill us."

The smirk returned to Alfie's gaze. "There's been a change of plans. We wanted to give you a chance to come to the dark side. Or the right side as we like to call it."

Kai practically snorted. "No way is that happening."

Alfie cocked his head. "Fine then. Have it your way."

Then shots began to fly through the air.

———

As gunfire sounded, Tori's heart lurched into her throat.

No! What if Kai had just been hurt? If any of them had been hurt?

She, Larchmont, and Trevor were skirting the edge of the trees, but the cabin was close enough to see. However, she had no idea what was happening behind those walls.

"Should we call for more backup?" Tori asked Larchmont.

He shook his head. "There's no time. Stay behind me, though, okay?"

She nodded even though she almost felt numb with panic.

"We don't know how many people might be inside. Could be one. It could be many more. But we need to be on guard. The element of surprise is going to be our friend. I don't think that whoever is inside will expect us to come back."

All she could think about was Kai. She imagined his lifeless body on the floor, and it nearly broke her heart to picture that.

Stay positive, she told herself. Thinking in worst-case scenarios won't get you anywhere.

A rumble of nerves swept through her. She was in way over her head right now.

Still, they crept forward. As they reached the edge of the woods, Larchmont nodded back at them.

When he motioned, they ran toward the cabin. Pressed themselves against the walls there.

Larchmont took the lead, Trevor behind him.

Tori gripped her gun with one hand and the defibrillator with the other.

She prayed she wouldn't have to use this, but she wanted it close, just in case.

As they approached the door, more gunfire rang out, followed by shouts.

Whatever was going on in there . . . it was bad. Really bad.

Even though she was terrified, she knew she had to get in there and help . . . before it was too late.

CHAPTER
FIFTY-FOUR

KAI PULLED the trigger before ducking back behind the door. This wall was the only thing that made him feel safe.

His bullets had already hit two of the men. The wounds hadn't killed them, but it had taken the men down.

Stephen stood behind Kai. Despite his injuries, he had his gun, and he'd fired as well.

It was only a matter of time before they ran out of ammunition. Then they'd have to fight the old-fashioned way.

Stephen wouldn't last long that way. His body was too weak.

That meant it would be Kai and Gage against four men.

They had to make sure their odds were a little more in their favor.

As one of the men reloaded his ammunition cartridge, Gage pulled the trigger.

His bullet hit the man in the shoulder and took him down.

Three against two now.

Then the gunfire stopped.

Kai paused as well.

What were they doing? Why were Alfie and his two other men simply staring at them?

What was their game plan?

As Alfie glanced at his phone and hit the screen, the truth hit Kai.

As he reached for his chest, everything around him went still.

His heart beat once. Twice.

Then nothing. His lungs froze

The room swirled around him, and he fell to the floor.

———

Tori peered inside in time to see Kai and Gage drop to the floor.

"No!" The word slipped out before she realized it.

Then it hit her what she'd done.

Alfie/Rocky and his men turned toward them, guns raised.

Larchmont and Trevor fired.

As they did, she ducked to the other side of the house.

She knew she was taking a risk, but she also knew that with every second that passed, Kai's and Gage's lives were on the line.

She had to do something!

She went to the back door and paused. Peered inside.

The men were turned away from her, meaning she was out of sight.

Tori had to get to Kai before it was too late.

She sucked in a breath and lifted a quick prayer.

She darted inside, still gripping that defibrillator.

She ran into the room where Kai laid on the floor.

Stephen knelt beside him, a questioning look on his face.

"I need to use the defibrillator on him," she said. "Can you help Gage? I know you're not up to full speed, but just do your best."

He nodded. Went to the door. Paused. Then he darted across the hall.

This was the best Tori could do right now. She only had one defibrillator.

Just as she'd done for Stephen last night, she

ripped open Kai's shirt. Grabbed the paddles. Booted up the machine.

Then she placed the paddles on Kai's chest and pressed the button to give his heart the electrical charge it needed.

After the first pulse went through him, she paused. Waited. Prayed.

Across the hall, she saw Stephen doing CPR on Gage. He needed her attention too. But if Stephen could just keep his heart beating for a couple more minutes.

Kai still lay on the floor.

Gunfire still flew through the air.

Danger still came from every direction.

She waited a moment and then tried again.

This time, the pulse worked.

Kai's eyes fluttered open.

Thank You, Jesus! Without thinking, she leaned forward and quickly pressed her lips against his forehead.

Then, wasting no more time, she darted across the hall.

Something was happening in the kitchen area. But she didn't have time to worry about what.

No, now she needed to make sure that Gage also stayed alive.

KAI'S THOUGHTS were fuzzy as he drank in deep breaths.

What had just happened?

Yet in the deep recesses of his mind, he knew. He was vaguely aware of everything that was going on.

But everything had gone silent around him.

Except for the sound of Tori's voice . . .

She was close.

She had kissed his forehead, hadn't she?

He almost wanted to smile at that thought.

Tori . . . how could he have been so foolish? He should have let her know how he was feeling right away. He had to stop hiding behind his past and his new position with the Shadow Agency.

Some things were more important than work. He

couldn't give his life to an organization that might drop him at the blink of an eye.

"I've got him!" Tori said.

He moved his head and tried to turn, but his hand went to his chest, which was still sore.

Through squinted eyes, he saw Gage begin to stir.

Good. His colleague should be okay.

He continued to turn until he could see down the hallway.

Larchmont was there, and he held a gun to Alfie. Four men lay on the ground. But there was still another one somewhere. Maybe out of sight? It was impossible to know.

In the distance, sirens began to wail.

Tori rushed back to Kai and knelt beside him.

The relief and concern on her face was obvious.

She placed her hands on both sides of his face as she peered down at him. "I'm so glad you're okay. I was so scared there for a while."

"I'm so glad you came."

"Now it's time for you guys to get the medical help you need. We can worry about being arrested later."

"Tori—" he started.

"It's going to be okay," she assured him.

As those words left her lips, he heard a thud as if something had hit the floor. Something big and heavy.

Tori looked up, and the sides of her eyes crinkled. "What . . . ?"

"What's going on?" Had someone else been hurt? Kai's thoughts raced.

"It's . . . Larchmont. He just fell to the floor."

She stood and ran down the hall toward the man.

Another thought hit Kai.

What if Larchmont had a device implanted inside him also?

———

Tori stood by Kai's bedside, waiting for him to fully wake up from his surgery. He was at a private medical facility in the West Virginia mountains. Larchmont had set things up here at the facility, and everyone had been brought here under FBI supervision.

The Shadow Agency guys had initially resisted until the special agent in charge—a man named Lucas—had shown them the correspondence he'd had with Larchmont.

They were all still cautious considering everything that happened.

Kai had just had the device near his heart removed.

As she'd promised, Tori stayed in the room during the procedure. She'd scrubbed in so she could observe everything. Nothing suspicious had happened.

She was so glad the device was gone. She could rest better at night knowing that. She did, however, have other concerns lingering in the back of her mind.

So much had happened.

Two days had passed since the showdown at the cabin.

Larchmont was still in intensive care here at the same facility. FBI agents were standing guard. Larchmont hadn't awoken, but his vitals had stabilized.

They had been told that he'd had a device implanted in him also.

Did that mean Larchmont had once been through the program as well? That was how it seemed.

Tori struggled with the questions, and she knew Kai and his colleagues did also.

But the team had other things to worry about. For starters, they were all having surgery to remove the devices near their hearts. Gage had gone first, and now Kai. A man named Austin would be next, followed by Trevor.

Yesterday, they'd found out the charges against her, Kai, and Gage had been dropped. They were no longer wanted for Landon's murder. Trevor had found the real security footage, which showed another man breaking into the house. That man happened to be one of the men who'd been shot at the cabin. He'd claimed no association with Monarch, however. Last Tori had heard, the man refused to give up the name of the person who'd hired him.

He was going to take the fall for what had happened—just like a good little soldier, she supposed.

Tori had a feeling he'd been directed to say that. And, of course, Monarch hadn't left any type of trail leading back to him—other than the fact that he'd hired private security.

The team still didn't know what exactly the man's connection was to all this. But they were still investigating and still determined to find answers.

Tori was extremely grateful her name had been cleared. At least prison time wasn't on her immediate list of concerns.

She'd been able to put together a better picture in her mind of what had happened.

Vintage had begun asking questions after some medical episodes. Those questions had led Vintage to the training facility up in Michigan. He'd then cross-referenced the addresses associated with that location, which had led him to the office the Shadow Agency had just opened in DC—and Kai.

He'd shared that information with Nathan. But before Vintage could do anything else with it, he'd died in the auto accident.

Nathan had been suspicious about his friend's death, so he'd picked up where Vintage left off.

That had led him to tracking down blueprints to several government and military facilities. It also led him to create a suspect list as to who he thought might be ultimately pulling the strings in the organization.

However, Nathan hadn't gotten very far in his investigation before he also died.

Kai stirred beside her, and she snapped her thoughts to him.

His eyes fluttered open, and he let out a long breath. He blinked some more, and Tori grabbed a cup of water so he could take a sip through the straw. After a few minutes, he appeared more lucid.

"Everything go okay?"

She nodded. "The device is gone. It's not a threat to you anymore."

"That's great news."

"It is." She still wasn't clear on who had actually activated the devices. Had it been Alfie? Or someone else doing so from a distance—Rafferty, perhaps?

The investigation was still underway.

Kai grasped her hand as she stood at his bedside. "Thank you for everything you've done."

"Are you sure you want to be thanking me?" Tori asked him, wry humor in her voice. "Just think how different your life would be if we had never met."

"We needed to address all the things you brought to our attention." His voice sounded hoarse but sincere. "I'm glad you found me."

She couldn't help but smile as she looked at him. "Despite everything we've been through, I'm glad that this broken road led me to you again, to quote a country song. At least, that *sounds* like it could be a country song."

He grinned.

As he did, their gazes caught, and something passed between them.

Tori could see in the depths of Kai's gaze that he cared about her. She cared about him too. Their experiences, experiences that normally might have driven them apart, had this time proven to pull them closer.

"They're going to let me go from here today, right?" Kai asked as he stared up at her from the bed.

"That's what I heard."

"Good. I want to take you to dinner."

She tilted her head in surprise. "Do you?"

His smile faded. "I do. But maybe after some of this settles down."

"Probably a good idea." Tori couldn't fault him for that. Striking up a romance in the middle of a situation like this just didn't seem wise.

But she could live with the promise that there was more to come. In fact, she preferred to go slow. In matters of the heart, she preferred caution.

He squeezed her hand harder. "Thank you again for everything you've done."

At his words, Tori leaned close and planted a light kiss on his forehead. "Of course."

They still had a lot of things to figure out. He worked in DC. Her home was in Florida. He still worked for the Shadow Agency. She needed to find another job—maybe in DC.

They could figure those things out later.

"I'm still curious about this facility." Kai glanced at the sterile room with state-of-the-art equipment. "How did Larchmont get us in here? What's his connection? Is the FBI on our side?"

As the words left his mouth, the door opened. "I might be able to help you answer some of those questions."

Tori looked up, and a woman she'd never seen before stood there. She was striking with white-blonde hair, a slender build, and a deep blue power suit with heels.

"Who are you?" Kai's hand clenched as if he wanted to reach for his gun. But he didn't have one nearby.

"Cynthia," the fifty-something woman answered cooly.

"Cynthia who?" Kai pressed, his voice suddenly stronger.

"Cynthia Larchmont . . . Alan's wife. And I'm going to be taking over until he recovers."

Tori's eyes widened, and she glanced at Kai.

This was clearly the first Kai had heard Larchmont was married.

All kinds of secrets were out there, weren't they?

And they were just beginning to peel back all the layers.

~~~

Thank you for reading *Shadow Collateral*. If you enjoyed this book, please consider leaving a review.

Coming next: *Shadow Survivor*!

~~~

ALSO BY CHRISTY BARRITT:

YOU ALSO MIGHT ENJOY:

LANTERN BEACH BLACKOUT

Dark Water

Colton Locke can't forget the black op that went terribly wrong. Desperate for a new start, he moves to Lantern Beach, North Carolina, and forms Blackout, a private security firm. Despite his hero status, he can't erase the mistakes he's made. For the past year, Elise Oliver hasn't been able to shake the feeling that there's more to her husband's death than she was told. When she finds a hidden box of his personal possessions, more questions—and suspicions—arise. The only person she trusts to help her is her husband's best friend, Colton Locke. Someone wants Elise dead. Is it because she knows too much? Or is it to keep her from finding the truth? The

Blackout team must uncover dark secrets hiding beneath seemingly still waters. But those very secrets might just tear the team apart.

Safe Harbor

Guilt over past mistakes haunts former Navy SEAL Dez Rodriguez. When he's asked to guard a pop star during a music festival on Lantern Beach, he's all set for what he hopes is a breezy assignment. Bree hasn't found fame to be nearly as fulfilling as she dreamed. Instead, she's more like a carefully crafted character living out a pre-scripted story. When a stalker's threats become deadly, her life—and career—are turned upside down. From the start, Bree sees her temporary bodyguard as a player, and Dez sees Bree as a spoiled rich girl. But when they're thrown together in a fight for survival, both must learn to trust. Can Dez protect Bree—and his carefully guarded heart? Or will their safe harbor ultimately become their death trap?

Ripple Effect

Griff McIntyre never expected his ex-wife and three-year-old daughter to come to Lantern Beach. After an abduction attempt, they're desperate for safety. Now Griff's not letting either of them out of his sight. Bethany knows Griff is the only one who can protect them, despite the fact that he broke her heart. But she'll do anything to keep her daughter safe—even if it means playing nicely with a man she can't stand. As peril ripples through their lives, Griff and Bethany must work together to protect their daughter. But an unseen enemy wants something from them . . . and will stop at nothing to get it. When disaster strikes, can Griff keep his family safe? Or will past mistakes bring the ultimate failure?

Rising Tide

Benjamin James knows there's a traitor within his former command. The rest of his team might even think it's him. As danger closes in, he must clear himself and stop a deadly plot by a dangerous terrorist group. All CJ Compton wanted was a new start after her career ended under suspicion. Working as the house manager for private security group Blackout seems perfect. But there's more trouble here than what she left behind. As the tide rushes in, the stakes continue to rise. If the Blackout team fails, it's not just Lantern Beach at stake—it's the whole country. Can Benjamin and CJ overcome their differences and work together to find the truth?

LANTERN BEACH BLACKOUT: THE NEW RECRUITS

Rocco

Former Navy SEAL and new Blackout recruit Rocco Foster is on a simple in and out mission. But the operation turns complicated when an unsuspecting woman wanders into the line of fire. Peyton Ellison's life mission is to sprinkle happiness on those around her. When a cupcake delivery turns into a fight for survival, she must trust her rescuer—a handsome stranger—to keep her safe. Rocco is determined to figure out why someone is targeting Peyton. First, he must keep the intriguing woman safe and earn her trust. But threats continue to pummel them as incriminating evidence emerges and pits them against each other. With time running out, the two must set aside both their growing attraction and their doubts about each other in order to work together. But the perilous facts they discover leave them wondering what exactly the truth is . . . and if the truth can be trusted.

Axel

Women are missing. Private security firm Blackout must find them before another victim disappears. Axel Hendrix likes to live on the edge. That's why being a Navy SEAL suited him so well. But after his last mission, he cut his losses and joined Blackout instead. His team's latest case involves an undercover investigation on Lantern Beach. Olivia Rollins came to the island to escape her problems—and danger. When trouble from her past shows up in town, she impulsively blurts she's engaged to Axel, the womanizing man she's seen while waitressing. Now, she may not be the only one in danger. So could Axel. Axel knows Olivia might be his chance to find answers and that acting like her fiancé is the perfect cover for his latest assignment. But he doesn't like throwing Olivia into the middle of such a dangerous situation. Nor is he comfortable with the feelings she stirs inside him. With Olivia's life—as well as both their hearts—on the line, Axel must uncover the truth and stop an evil plan before more lives are destroyed.

Beckett

When the daughter of a federal judge is abducted, private security firm Blackout must find her. Psychologist Samantha Reynolds doesn't know why someone is targeting her. Even after a risky mission to save her, danger still lingers. She's determined to use her insights into the human mind to help decode the deadly clues being left in the wake of her rescue. Former Navy SEAL Beckett Jones needs to figure out who's responsible for the crimes hounding Sami. He's not sure why he's so protective of the woman he rescued, but he'll do anything to keep her safe—even if it means risking his heart. As the body count rises, there's no room for error. Beckett and Sami must both tear down the careful walls they've built around themselves in order to survive. If they don't figure out who's responsible, the madman will continue his death spree . . . and one of them might be next.

Gabe

When former Navy SEAL and current Blackout operative Gabe Michaels is almost killed in a hit-and-run, the aftermath completely upends his life. He's no longer safe—and he's not the only one. Dr. Autumn Spenser came to Lantern Beach to start fresh. But while treating Gabe after his accident, she senses there's more to what happened to him than meets the eye. When she digs deeper into his past, she never expects to be drawn into a deadly dilemma. Gabe has been infatuated with the pretty doctor since the day they met. Now, can he keep her from harm? Could someone out of his league ever return his feelings or will her past hurts keep them apart? As danger continues to pummel them, Gabe and Autumn are thrown together in a quest to find answers. More important than their growing attraction, they must stay alive long enough to stop the person desperate to destroy them.

LANTERN BEACH BLACKOUT: DANGER RISING

Brandon

Physically he's protecting her. But emotionally she's never felt more exposed. The last person tech heiress Finley Cooper ever wanted to see again was Brandon Hale. Two years ago, Brandon shattered her heart. Now Finley needs protection, and, against her wishes, Brandon is assigned the job. Even worse, they must pretend to be a couple in order to find answers. Brandon, a former Navy SEAL, met Finley while on an undercover assignment in Ecuador. But he broke her trust, and now he doesn't blame Finley for hating him. As a new Blackout operative, Brandon's first assignment throws him into Finley's life 24/7. Someone wants her dead, and it's clear this person won't stop until that mission is accomplished. To keep her safe, Brandon must regain Finley's trust. Can he convince her she's more than a job to him? Or will peril permanently silence them?

Dylan

His job is to protect her. The trouble is . . . she doesn't want protection. Former Navy SEAL Dylan Granger's new assignment requires him to use both his tactical abilities and his acting skills. Hired by Katie Logan's father, his job is to protect the gutsy university professor while concealing his identity. To maintain his cover, he takes the unassuming role of her new assistant. Katie—a disgraced reporter—has stumbled upon a lead she can't ignore. Now it's clear someone is targeting her, but she refuses to back down. Her handsome new assistant is a welcome distraction from the chaos. But Dylan's skillset goes way beyond his job description, and Katie begins to suspect there's more to Dylan than he's letting on. Dylan's mission can't be disclosed—not if he wants to keep Katie safe. But as his feelings for her grow and the danger increases, keeping his secret becomes more of a challenge than he ever imagined. With innocent lives on the line, Dylan must choose between protecting Katie or savings others.

Maddox

He's on the case . . . and she's his prime suspect. Classified technology is missing, a delivery driver is dead, and former Navy SEAL Maddox King must find the culprits before a dangerous plan is enacted. To find answers, the Blackout agent must go undercover as a maintenance man at millionaire Seymore Whitlock's estate. While there, he sets his sights on Whitlock's personal assistant, Taryn Parsons, a woman who has everything to gain and nothing to lose. Six months ago, Whitlock plucked Taryn out of obscurity to become his caretaker. But with deadly incidents haunting the estate, Taryn doesn't know who she can trust—including the new maintenance man who is both intriguing . . . and unnerving. The stakes continue to escalate, and Maddox is running out of time to find answers. With the body count rising along with his list of suspects, this assignment may be his most challenging yet . . . for both his skillset and his heart.

Titus

She shattered his heart once. Can he set her betrayal aside for the sake of his country? The last person Titus Armstrong wants to join forces with is the woman who dumped him for his brother, Alex. But Presley Lennox is Blackout's best chance at infiltrating a dangerous organization known as The System and finding out more about their deadly plans. Presley Lennox wants out—of both an abusive relationship and the radical group she's become entangled with because of Alex. When Titus reappears in her life, he's like an answer to prayer—until he asks her to dive deeper into the very life she's been trying to escape. A dangerous plan is brewing that could destroy thousands of lives. Titus and Presley may be the only ones who can stop what's about to be unleashed. Failure would mean certain chaos . . . not only for them but for their nation.

ABOUT THE AUTHOR

USA Today has called Christy Barritt's books "scary, funny, passionate, and quirky."

Christy writes both mystery and romantic suspense novels that are clean with underlying messages of faith. Her books have sold more than four million copies and have won the Daphne du Maurier Award for Excellence in Suspense and Mystery, have been twice nominated for the Romantic Times Reviewers' Choice Award, and have finaled for both a Carol Award and Foreword Magazine's Book of the Year.

She is married to her Prince Charming, a man who thinks she's hilarious—but only when she's not trying to be. Christy is a self-proclaimed klutz, an avid music lover who's known for spontaneously bursting into song, and a road trip aficionado.

When she's not working or spending time with her family, she enjoys singing, playing the guitar, and exploring small, unsuspecting towns where people have no idea how accident-prone she is.

Find Christy online at:
www.christybarritt.com
www.facebook.com/christybarritt
www.twitter.com/cbarritt

Sign up for Christy's newsletter to get information on all of her latest releases here: **www.christybarritt. com/newsletter-sign-up/**

facebook.com/AuthorChristyBarritt
x.com/christybarritt
instagram.com/cebarritt

COMPLETE BOOK LIST

Squeaky Clean Mysteries
#1 Hazardous Duty
Half Witted (Squeaky Clean In Between Mysteries
Book 1, novella)
#2 Suspicious Minds
#2.5 It Came Upon a Midnight Crime (novella)
Half Truth (Squeaky Clean In Between Mysteries
Book 2, novella)
#3 Organized Grime
#4 Dirty Deeds
#5 The Scum of All Fears
#6 To Love, Honor and Perish
#7 Mucky Streak
#8 Foul Play
#9 Broom & Gloom
#10 Dust and Obey

#11 Thrill Squeaker
#11.5 Swept Away (novella)
#12 Cunning Attractions
#13 Cold Case: Clean Getaway
#14 Cold Case: Clean Sweep
#15 Cold Case: Clean Break
#16 Cleans to an End
While You Were Sweeping, A Riley Thomas Spinoff

The Sierra Files

#1 Pounced
#2 Hunted
#3 Pranced
#4 Rattled

Lantern Beach Mysteries

#1 Hidden Currents
#2 Flood Watch
#3 Storm Surge
#4 Dangerous Waters
#5 Perilous Riptide
#6 Deadly Undertow

Lantern Beach Romantic Suspense

#1 Tides of Deception
#2 Shadow of Intrigue
#3 Storm of Doubt
#4 Winds of Danger

#5 Rains of Remorse
#6 Torrents of Fear

Lantern Beach P.D.
#1 On the Lookout
#2 Attempt to Locate
#3 First Degree Murder
#4 Dead on Arrival
#5 Plan of Action

Lantern Beach Escape
Afterglow (a novelette)

Lantern Beach Blackout
#1 Dark Water
#2 Safe Harbor
#3 Ripple Effect
#4 Rising Tide

Lantern Beach Guardians
#1 Hide and Seek
#2 Shock and Awe
#3 Safe and Sound

Lantern Beach Blackout: The New Recruits
#1 Rocco
#2 Axel
#3 Beckett

#4 Gabe

Lantern Beach Mayday
#1 Run Aground
#2 Dead Reckoning
#3 Tipping Point

Lantern Beach Christmas
Silent Night

Lantern Beach Blackout: Danger Rising
#1 Brandon
#2 Dylan
#3 Maddox
#4 Titus

Beach Bound Books and Beans Mysteries
#1 Bound by Murder
#2 Bound by Disaster
#3 Bound by Mystery
#4 Bound by Trouble
#5 Bound by Mayhem

Lantern Beach Exposure
#1 Fractured Lies
#2 Shattered Whispers
#3 Unsteady Ground
#4 Troubled Graves

#5 Deceptive Shallows
#6 Secret Shores

True Crime Junkies
#1 Just the Nicest Person
#2 He Walks Among Us
#3 Never Happen to You
#4 The Dead of Night
#5 Leave the Lights On
#6 The End of the Road
#7 The Secrets She Kept
#8 Most Likely to Die

The Shadow Agency
#1 Shadow Operative
#2 Shadow Chaser
#3 Shadow Assignment
#4 Shadow Collateral
#5 Shadow Survivor

Fog Lake Suspense
#1 Edge of Peril
#2 Margin of Error
#3 Brink of Danger
#4 Line of Duty
#5 Legacy of Lies
#6 Secrets of Shame
#7 Refuge of Redemption

Vanishing Ranch
#1 Forgotten Secrets
#2 Necessary Risk
#3 Risky Ambition
#4 Deadly Intent
#5 Lethal Betrayal
#6 High Stakes Deception
#7 Fatal Vendetta
#8 Troubled Tidings
#9 Narrow Escape
#10 Desperate Rescue

Saltwater Cowboys
#1 Saltwater Cowboy
#2 Breakwater Protector
#3 Cape Corral Keeper
#4 Seagrass Secrets
#5 Driftwood Danger
#6 Unwavering Security

Beach House Mysteries
#1 The Cottage on Ghost Lane
#2 The Inn on Hanging Hill
#3 The House on Dagger Point
#4 The Bungalow on Shadow Road

The Worst Detective Ever
#1 Ready to Fumble

#2 Reign of Error
#3 Safety in Blunders
#4 Join the Flub
#5 Blooper Freak
Raven Remington Relentless
#6 Flaw Abiding Citizen
#7 Gaffe Out Loud
#8 Joke and Dagger
#9 Wreck the Halls
#10 Glitch and Famous
#11 Not on My Botch
#12 One Hit Blunder

Holly Anna Paladin Mysteries
#1 Random Acts of Murder
#2 Random Acts of Deceit
#2.5 Random Acts of Scrooge
#3 Random Acts of Malice
#4 Random Acts of Greed
#5 Random Acts of Fraud
#6 Random Acts of Outrage
#7 Random Acts of Iniquity

Cape Thomas Series
#1 Dubiosity
#2 Disillusioned
#3 Distorted

Carolina Moon Series
#1 Home Before Dark
#2 Gone By Dark
#3 Wait Until Dark
#4 Light the Dark
#5 Taken By Dark

The Sidekick's Survival Guide
#1 The Art of Eavesdropping
#2 The Perks of Meddling
#3 The Exercise of Interfering
#4 The Practice of Prying
#5 The Skill of Snooping
#6 The Craft of Being Covert

School of Hard Rocks Mysteries
#1 The Treble with Murder
#2 Crime Strikes a Chord
#3 Tone Death

Standalone Romantic Suspense
Keeping Guard
The Last Target
Race Against Time
Ricochet
Key Witness
Lifeline
High-Stakes Holiday Reunion

Desperate Measures
Hidden Agenda
Mountain Hideaway
Dark Harbor
Shadow of Suspicion
The Baby Assignment
The Cradle Conspiracy
Trained to Defend
Mountain Survival
Dangerous Mountain Rescue
Lethal Mountain Pursuit

Crime á la Mode Mysteries
#1 Dead Man's Float
#2 Milkshake Up
#3 Bomb Pop Threat
#4 Banana Split Personalities

Standalone Novels
Vacation Friends
Death of the Couch Potato's Wife
Imperfect
The Good Girl
The Wrecking

Standalone Sweet Christmas Novellas
Home to Chestnut Grove
How Her Ex Stole Christmas

The Gabby St. Claire Diaries (a Tween Mystery series)

#1 The Curtain Call Caper
#2 The Disappearing Dog Dilemma
#3 The Bungled Bike Burglaries

Nonfiction

Characters in the Kitchen
Changed: True Stories of Finding God through Christian Music (out of print)
The Novel in Me: The Beginner's Guide to Writing and Publishing a Novel (out of print)

www.ingramcontent.com/pod-product-compliance
Lightning Source LLC
Chambersburg PA
CBHW021334150726
47989CB00005B/1976